Kira opened the manila folder and took out the newspaper article from the Denver Post.

It was a small piece about two Montana men—one an off-duty police officer and the other a Northbridge business owner—who had rushed into a burning house to rescue a family trapped inside. The two men had saved the family and then had gone back in for the pets only to have a beam knock Addison Walker unconscious and break Cutler Grant's ankle. Still, Officer Grant had managed to drag the unconscious businessman to safety.

The name Addison Walker meant nothing to Kira.

But Cutler Grant—that was something else. Kira knew a *Cutty Grant.*

Could it be the same man who held the truth about her long-lost sister? Whether this would turn out to be a wild-goose chase or she was about to embark on an adventure with destiny, Kira had to find the injured cop. She owed it to her family and to herself.

Bottom line: this man was her only hope.

Dear Reader,

We're smack in the middle of summer, which can only mean long, lazy days at the beach. And do we have some fantastic books for you to bring along! We begin this month with a new continuity, only in Special Edition, called THE PARKS EMPIRE, a tale of secrets and lies, love and revenge. And Laurie Paige opens the series with *Romancing the Enemy*. A schoolteacher who wants to avenge herself against the man who ruined her family decides to move next door to the man's son. But things don't go exactly as planned, as she finds herself falling…for the enemy.

Stella Bagwell continues her MEN OF THE WEST miniseries with *Her Texas Ranger,* in which an officer who's come home to investigate a murder fins complications in the form of the girl he loved in high school. Victoria Pade begins her NORTHBRIDGE NUPTIALS miniseries, revolving around a town famed for its weddings, with *Babies in the Bargain*. When a woman hoping to reunite with her estranged sister finds instead her widowed husband and her children, she winds up playing nanny to the whole crew. Can wife and mother be far behind? THE KENDRICKS OF CAMELOT by Christine Flynn concludes with *Prodigal Prince Charming,* in which a wealthy playboy tries to help a struggling caterer with her business and becomes much more than just her business partner in the process. Brand-new author Mary J. Forbes debuts with *A Forever Family,* featuring a single doctor dad and the woman he hires to work for him. And the men of the CHEROKEE ROSE miniseries by Janis Reams Hudson continues with *The Other Brother,* in which a woman who always contend her handsome neighbor as one of her best friends suddenly finds herself looking at him in a new light.

Happy reading! And come back next month for six new fabulous books, all from Silhouette Special Edition.

Gail Chasan
Senior Editor

Please address questions and book requests to:
Silhouette Reader Service
U.S.: 3010 Walden Ave., P.O. Box 1325, Buffalo, NY 14269
Canadian: P.O. Box 609, Fort Erie, Ont. L2A 5X3

Babies in the Bargain

VICTORIA PADE

Silhouette

SPECIAL EDITION

Published by Silhouette Books

America's Publisher of Contemporary Romance

SILHOUETTE BOOKS

ISBN 0-373-24623-4

BABIES IN THE BARGAIN

This edition published by arrangement with Harlequin Books S.A.

® and TM are trademarks of Harlequin Books S.A., used under license. Trademarks indicated with ® are registered in the United States Patent and Trademark Office, the Canadian Trade Marks Office and in other countries.

Visit Silhouette Books at www.eHarlequin.com

Printed in U.S.A.

Books by Victoria Pade

Silhouette Special Edition

*A Ranching Family
†Baby Times Three
**Northbridge Nuptials

Silhouette Books

World's Most Eligible Bachelors
Wyoming Wrangler

Montana Mavericks:
  Wed in Whitehorn
The Marriage Bargain

The Coltons
From Boss to Bridegroom

VICTORIA PADE

is a bestselling author of both historical and contemporary romance fiction, and mother of two energetic daughters, Cori and Erin. Although she enjoys her chosen career as a novelist, she occasionally laments that she has never traveled farther from her Colorado home than Disneyland, instead spending all her spare time plugging away at her computer. She takes breaks from writing by indulging in her favorite hobby—eating chocolate.

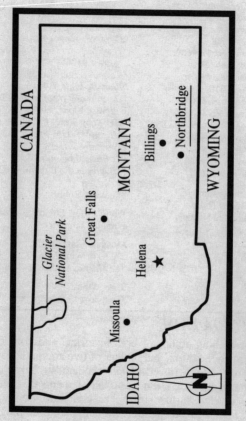

CANADA

*Glacier
National Park*

Great Falls •

MONTANA

Billings •

• Northbridge

Helena
★

Missoula •

IDAHO

N

WYOMING

All underlined places are fictitious.

Chapter One

Darkness hadn't completely fallen when Kira Wentworth drove from farm-and-ranch land into the city proper of Northbridge, Montana, on Wednesday night. Still, most of the stores and shops that lined the small college town's main thoroughfare were closed. Even the gas station was being locked up as she pulled into the lot.

"Excuse me," Kira said from the window of her rental car to the attendant as he removed the key from the door and pocketed it. "Can I bother you for directions?"

"Nothin's hard to find in Northbridge," the teenage boy informed her as if she was asking a dumb question.

He did come to the side of her car, though.

"I'm looking for one-o-four Jellison Street," she informed him.

The freckle-faced teenager didn't have to think about it before he said, "That's the Grant place. Officer Grant is laid up with a broken ankle so he should be there."

The teenager gave her brief instructions. Then, without another word, he rounded her car to go to the single island and padlock the nozzle on the only gas pump.

"Thank you," Kira called after him.

"Sure," he answered, taking off on foot and leaving her behind without a second glance.

Kira rolled up the car window again and turned the air conditioner higher. Just the thought that she was within three blocks of her destination increased her stress level and made her hotter than even the mid-July temperature warranted.

Hoping the heat and the drive through the open countryside hadn't made her look too much the worse for wear, she glanced at herself in the rearview mirror before heading out of the gas station.

Her mascara hadn't left smudges around her blue eyes, and light mauve lipstick still stained lips that weren't too thin or too thick. But despite the fact that she'd reapplied blush in the Billings Airport when she'd landed, her skin looked pale again.

"It might not even be the same guy," she reminded her reflection. "This could still be a wild-goose chase."

But the reminder didn't help much. She continued

to feel as if she had butterflies in the pit of her stomach, and if the pallor of her skin wasn't enough, there was further proof of her nervousness in the fact that somewhere during the drive from Billings she'd tucked her hair behind her ears—a habit her father had detested.

She hurriedly took a comb from her purse—as if Tom Wentworth might appear at any moment to punish her for the infraction—running it through the precision-cut, shoulder-length, straight honey-blond hair until every strand was right where it belonged.

Then she replaced the comb, reapplied blush to her high cheekbones, tugged at the collar of her white blouse to make sure it was exactly centered at her throat and plucked a single string from the right leg of her navy-blue slacks.

Not perfect, she judged as she took another look at herself in the mirror, but at least she was presentable and it was the best she could do under the circumstances.

She noticed then that the clock on the dashboard read five minutes after nine and it occurred to her that she probably shouldn't waste any more time. She didn't know much about small-town life, but if even the gas station was closed already, maybe everyone went to bed early, too. And she didn't want to risk having to wait another day to find out what she'd come to find out.

She put the sedan back into gear and pulled out of the station, taking a right at the only stoplight, and then a quick left after that onto Jellison.

What she found there was a nice neighborhood shaded with tall elm, oak and maple trees lining the street on both sides. Beyond the trees at the curb were medium-size frame houses that looked as if they'd all been pressed through the same cookie cutter in 1950.

The two-story, wedding-cake-shaped houses with the covered front porches were distinguished from one another only by the different earth-tone colors they'd been painted, the outside shutters and flower boxes that had been added to several of them, and the yards—some with elaborate landscaping and others with only well-tended lawns.

The address she was looking for came into view on the fourth house from the corner—that one had tan siding, white shutters and a wooden swing hanging from chains on the left side of the porch.

There was a black-and-white SUV parked in the driveway with Northbridge Police stenciled on the sides and back. There weren't any cars parked in front, though, so Kira pulled to a stop at the curb.

Before she turned off the engine she took the manila folder from the passenger seat and opened it. Inside was the newspaper article from Sunday's *Denver Post* that she'd cut out and laminated.

It was a small piece about two Montana men—one an off-duty police officer and the other a Northbridge business owner—who had rushed into a burning house to rescue a family trapped inside. The two men had saved the family and then had gone back in for the pets only to have a beam knock Addison Walker unconscious and break Cutler Grant's ankle. Still, Officer Grant had managed to drag the unconscious businessman to safety.

The name Addison Walker meant nothing to Kira.

But Cutler Grant—that was something else. Kira knew—sort of—a *Cutty* Grant.

There wasn't much information about the two men in the pictureless piece, but it did say that Cutler Grant was a widower with eighteen-month-old twin daughters.

That was a surprise. The *Cutty* Grant Kira knew had married her older sister and they'd had a son. A son who would be twelve years old by now.

So maybe this really was a wild-goose chase and the Cutler Grant in the newspaper wasn't the same Cutty Grant she knew.

But what she was hoping was that this *was* the same man. That she'd find out that the wife who had left him a widower with eighteen-month-old twins was his second wife. And that he would be able to tell Kira where to find Marla and their twelve-year-old son.

Kira put the slip of paper neatly back into the folder and replaced it on the passenger seat.

Then she turned off the car.

Ignoring the tension that tightened her shoulders, Kira picked up her leather purse and took it with her as she got out.

The scent of honeysuckle was in the air as she headed for the door. Light shone through the windows of the lower floor and the front door was open—probably to let in the cooler evening air—so apparently the occupants of 104 Jellison Street were still awake.

She climbed five cement steps to the porch. As she approached the door she could see through the screen. There was a man sitting on an antique chair, talking on the phone.

He caught sight of her, and without missing a beat, he motioned for her to come inside.

Who did he think she was? Kira wondered, staying rooted to that spot, unsure whether or not to actually go inside.

Although his looks had matured, she could tell that this man was the Cutty Grant she was looking for. But she knew there was no way he recognized her. The one and only time he'd seen her had lasted a total of ten minutes before she'd been dispatched to her room. Besides, she looked completely different than she had then.

But when she remained on the porch, he motioned to her even more insistently, and she didn't know what to do but oblige him. So she opened the screen and went in.

"Betty, we'll be okay," he was saying into the phone. "Family comes first. You have to take care of your mother."

Kira didn't want to appear to be listening so she kept her eyes on the floor. The floor where he had one foot stretched out in front of him. One big, bare foot with a white cast cupping his heel and disappearing under the leg of a pair of time-aged blue jeans that hugged a thigh thick enough to be noteworthy.

She tried to keep control of her eyes but they seemed to have a mind of their own and continued up to the plain white crew-neck T-shirt that fit him like a second skin and left no doubt that he was in good enough shape to have dragged a full-grown man out of a burning building. His chest and shoulders were that substantial, bulging with toned muscles. And his biceps were so big they stretched the short sleeves of the T-shirt to the limit.

"No, don't do that."

For a split-second Kira thought he might be talking to her, and she glanced quickly to his face.

But he was still talking into the phone. "You can't take care of things here and take care of your mom, too," he said.

In fact he wasn't even looking in Kira's direction. His focus really was on the floor where hers had begun, and he didn't seem aware that Kira's gaze was on his face now. Somehow that made it more difficult to lower her eyes and instead she was left studying the changes in him.

The seventeen-year-old boy she remembered had been cute enough to make her jealous of her older sister. Yet the boy was nothing compared to the man.

The grown-up Cutty Grant had the same sable-colored hair only now he wore it short all over and messy on top rather than long and shaggy.

It wasn't only his haircut that had changed. His face had gone from boyishly appealing to ruggedly striking. His very square forehead had become strong. His distinctive jawline and straight, slightly longish nose were more defined, and every angle and plane of his face seemed more sharply cut.

His upper lip was still narrow above a fuller bottom lip, and when he smiled at something the person on the other end of the phone said, two grooves bracketed either side of that mouth, which had gained a certain suppleness. And an indescribable sexiness, too.

His deep-set eyes hadn't undergone any alteration with age—they were still a remarkable shade of green unlike any other eyes Kira had ever seen. Dark green, the color of Christmas trees. Evergreen trees. And all in all, Kira thought that she'd never even met a man as head-turningly handsome as the adult Cutty Grant.

"Yes, the place is a mess, but Lucinda had no business reporting that to you," he said then.

Kira needed an excuse to tear her eyes away from him and that gave it to her. She forced herself to look from him into the living room.

She didn't know about the rest of the place but that room was definitely in disarray. There were toys on the floor, on the end tables, on the brown tweed sofa, even on the desk in the corner. There were children's clothes strewn here and there, including one tiny pair of pink shorts hanging over the lampshade of a pole lamp in the corner. There were unused diapers spilling from a sack on top of the television in the entertainment center. There was a plate with the crusts of a sandwich left on it, a half-empty glass of milk, and another smaller glass overturned in a puddle of orange juice on the oak coffee table. And there was just an overall air of clutter everywhere that sparked an urge in the meticulous Kira to put it all in order.

But of course she resisted that urge.

"I mean it, Betty. Forget about us until she's better. The girls and I will manage."

Kira noticed then that there was even debris on the stairs—more toys, more baby clothes, a sock that must have belonged to Cutty, and it occurred to her that no matter what he was telling the person he was talking to, he wasn't managing very well.

But in spite of that he insisted, "Really, you don't have to come by here in the morning before you pick up your mom from the hospital—"

There was a pause while the person on the other end interrupted him to say something, and whatever it was it apparently convinced him because he sighed and said, "Okay, but then that's it. An hour tomorrow morning. After that, I don't want to see you around here until your mom is a hundred percent better. If nothing else I'll get Ad over to help."

Whoever he was talking to said something that made Cutty Grant laugh a deep, throaty laugh that sounded so good it was almost sinful.

Then he said, "Yeah, I know, Ad isn't any more domestic than I am, but he can get more done with a bump on the head than I can with a bum ankle that's supposed to be elevated all the time. Just don't worry about it. Now I have to go. I have company. I'll see you in the morning. But only for an hour," he added, slowly enunciating each word for emphasis before he said goodbye.

The minute he hung up he turned his attention to Kira. "Sorry about that. That was the woman who usually helps me out around here with the babies and the housekeeping. Her mother herniated a disc in her back and she's fretting about leaving me in the lurch. She knows I'm not good for much when I'm supposed to stay off the foot," he said, pointing to his injured ankle.

Kira watched him stand and take a cane that was braced against the wall beside him.

Even leaning his weight on the cane he still stood at least six foot two and if Kira had thought his physique was impressive when he was sitting down, it was even more impressive when he was upright. There was definitely nothing boyish in that big, powerful tower of a man and it left Kira slightly dumbstruck.

Not that he seemed to notice as he continued. "So. Here you are. I could have sworn we said Thursday night between eight and nine to make sure the babies were asleep or I wouldn't have returned Betty's phone call."

That brought Kira to her senses. "Who do you think I am?"

"The journalism student from the college who's doing the article on Ad and me. Isn't that who you are?"

That explained why he'd waved her in.

Kira shook her head. "I'm not from the college," she said. "I'm Kira Wentworth. Marla's sister."

That sobered him instantly. In fact, it pulled his

amazing face into a frown that put two vertical creases between his eyebrows.

"Oh."

All the animation had drained from his voice and he didn't say anything for so long that Kira felt inclined to fill the silence with the reason for her sudden appearance on his doorstep.

"The Denver newspaper ran a little article about you and the other man saving a family from their burning house. It was the first time I had any clue about where Marla might be since the two of you left thirteen years ago. I'm here looking for her."

Cutty Grant closed his green eyes and Kira saw his jaw tense before he opened them again and sighed a sigh that sounded resigned but not happy.

He pointed toward the living room and said, "Let's go in there and sit."

Solemn. Kira knew whatever he was going to tell her couldn't be good, and her grip on her purse turned white-knuckle as she did as he'd suggested and went into the living room that looked as if a cyclone had hit it.

"Please. Sit," he repeated when she went on standing even then.

Kira conceded, passing up the littered sofa to remove a rag doll from the Bentley rocking chair that was at a forty-five-degree angle to the couch. She kept hold of the doll with her arms wrapped tightly around it, hugging it close as Cutty Grant joined her, sitting on the only clear spot on the sofa and raising his casted foot to a pillow on the coffee table in front of it.

For what seemed like an eternity he didn't speak, though. Or even look at her. Instead he kept his eyes on the cane, balancing it across his legs like a bridge.

And in the silence it occurred to Kira that although she'd seen signs of infants and of Cutty himself, she hadn't seen anything that would lead her to think her sister or her nephew were a part of the equation here. But she still hoped against hope that Cutty Grant was going to tell her he and Marla had divorced, that Marla had taken their son somewhere else, that he was a widower with two daughters because his second wife had died....

But the minute he said, "I'm sorry," Kira knew better and her heart sank. There was just something so ominous in his voice.

"Marla and I had a little boy," he told her then. "Your parents knew that so you must have, too."

"I knew you'd had a boy, yes," Kira confirmed tentatively, as if, if she hedged, it might not make the worst true.

"Then you probably knew he was autistic."

That surprised her. "No, I didn't know that. I only knew Marla had had a son because I overheard my mother telling my father when the baby was born. They never told me directly—she was so thoroughly disowned that I wasn't even to mention her name— and after that I never heard them talk about her or the baby again."

"There was an *after that*—" Disgust rang in his

tone but he seemed to reconsider what he'd been about to say and changed course. "Anthony. We named him Anthony."

It was unabashed pain that Kira heard in Cutty's voice then. Pain that etched his handsome face.

"I'm really hoping this isn't as bad as it seems," she said when he let another long silence pass.

Cutty Grant took a deep breath and shook his head to let her know in advance that her hopes were to no avail. "Seventeen months ago, it was February but we were having springlike weather, so Marla took Anthony into the front yard to get some fresh air. I don't really know why, but for some reason Anthony ran between two cars that were parked at the curb. There was a truck coming. Going faster than it should have been. The driver didn't see Anthony. Or Marla running after him..."

It was difficult for Cutty to say what he was saying, and after another pause he finally finished. "The truck hit them both."

Kira hadn't been prepared to hear that. Intellectually she'd realized that it was possible it was her sister who had left Cutty Grant a widower, but she hadn't really believed it was true.

"Marla is dead?" she whispered.

"I'm sorry."

"And Anthony?"

"He was killed instantly."

Through the tears that sprang to her eyes, Kira saw moisture gathering in those of the man across from her, too. But still she couldn't help the accusing tone when she said, "And you didn't let us know?"

A flash of anger dried his eyes and when he answered her it was barely contained in his own voice. "Marla lived a few hours after the accident and one of the few things she said to me during the time she was conscious was that she didn't want me to call her father. That she didn't want him here. Even if she didn't make it. I respected her wishes." And it was clear that he'd had no desire himself to bring Tom Wentworth into the picture.

"But *I* would have wanted to know," Kira said quietly as she lost the battle to hold back her own tears and they began to trail down her face.

Cutty Grant got up and limped out of the room, returning with a box of tissues that he held out for her.

Kira accepted one, thanking him perfunctorily and wiping her eyes as she struggled with the complex emotions running through her.

"I'm sorry," he repeated, setting the tissue box on the coffee table and sitting down once more. "If it's any consolation, not seeing you again after we eloped was the one thing Marla regretted."

It wasn't much consolation. It didn't take away all the years of missing Marla. Of wondering where she was. Of wishing she would call or write. Of longing to see her again, to be sisters again. It didn't take away all the time since Kira had grown up and been out on her own when she'd wanted so badly to have

Marla in her life and not had any way of knowing where she was.

"I tried to find her," Kira said through her tears, not really understanding why it was suddenly important to her that he know. "My parents said they didn't have any idea where she was—"

"That was a lie."

Kira had suspected as much but she couldn't force them to tell her.

She didn't say that to Cutty, though. She just continued. "I went to three private investigators but I couldn't afford their fees. I even tried different things on the Internet. But no matter what I did, I came up empty." As empty as she'd felt so much of the time after Marla had left. "I know we weren't related by blood, but she was still my sister. We shared a room from the time I was three years old. And, I don't know, I guess rather than being rivals or fighting with each other, we sort of banded together..." Kira's voice trailed off before she said too much.

But Cutty picked up the ball where she'd dropped it and said, "Does your father know you're here now?"

Kira finally managed to stop the flow of tears and dabbed at her face with the tissue. "He and my mom were killed a year ago in a freak accident. They were coming home from a day in the mountains when there was a rock slide onto the road. They were hit by a boulder that came right down on the car. They both died instantly."

"I'm sorry," he said once more. "Your mother was a nice enough woman."

That was true. It was just that *nice* hadn't had any potency against the strong will of the man she'd married. The man who had adopted her three-year-old daughter.

But that seemed beside the point now. Kira had come here hoping to find the sister she'd so desperately wanted to reconnect with. Hoping to find family. And it suddenly struck her that the only chance of that might be in Cutty Grant's twins.

"The article said you have eighteen-month-old daughters," she said then.

"Upstairs asleep as we speak," he confirmed, a brighter note edging his voice at the mere mention of them.

"Marla's babies?"

"Yes. They were barely three weeks old when the accident happened."

"My nieces," Kira said, trying it on for size because blood or no blood, if they were Marla's babies, Kira felt a connection to them.

"I guess so," Cutty conceded.

"I'd like to meet them. Get to know them. Would you let me?" she said impulsively and without any idea how she might go about that.

Cutty's frown from earlier reappeared and he didn't jump at the idea. Instead he said, "Like I said, they're asleep."

"I know. But…"

And that was when, completely out of the blue, the

mess in the room caught her attention again and an idea popped into her head.

"What if I took the place of that woman you were talking to on the phone a few minutes ago?" she said before the notion had even had a chance to ferment.

"Betty? What if you took Betty's place?" He sounded confused and leery at the same time.

"You said she took care of the twins and helped around the house, and without her—and with you needing to stay off your ankle—you're obviously in a bind. So what if I did it? I'd like to help and that way I could get to know the babies. Bond with them."

The more Kira considered this, the better it sounded to her.

But from the look on Cutty's face it wasn't having the same effect on him.

"Don't you have a job or a husband or a boyfriend or something you need to get back to?"

"No, I don't. In May I finished my Ph.D. in microbiology. I'm going to start teaching at the University of Colorado for the fall semester, but that doesn't begin until the last week in August. I wasn't really sure what I was going to do with myself until then but that means I'm free."

"No husband or boyfriend, either?" he asked, and Kira couldn't tell if he was looking for an out for himself or satisfying his own curiosity.

"No, no husband or boyfriend. I have one really close friend—Kit—but she can get along without me.

Plus she'll bring in my mail and water my plants for me, so it won't be any problem for me to stay.''

''You really want to spend your summer vacation picking up after us? Changing diapers?'' Cutty asked skeptically.

''I really do,'' she said, hating that she sounded as desperate as she felt. ''I admit that I don't have any experience with kids,'' she confessed because it seemed only fair to let him know what he was getting into. ''But when it comes to cleaning—''

''You're Tom Wentworth's daughter,'' Cutty supplied. ''I don't know, I like things casual.''

''Casual is good. I can be casual.'' Although she wasn't quite sure what *casual* housekeeping and child care meant.

But still he didn't look convinced. In fact, he looked downright dubious and as if he was on the verge of saying thanks, but no thanks.

Why would he, though? It was clear he needed help and she was offering it.

Unless maybe he still harbored resentment toward her family for the way things had played out that night thirteen years ago when he'd come with Marla to tell their parents that he'd gotten their seventeen-year-old daughter pregnant.

''You know,'' Kira ventured, ''I didn't have anything to do with what went on between you and my father. I know how ugly it got. He sent me to my room but I was hiding on the stairs, listening to what went on. He was a difficult man—''

''That's an understatement. He was a tyrant.''

Kira didn't dispute that. "But nobody can change the past and now he's gone and so is Marla. But there are your twins. And me. I lost all these years that I could have had with Marla, with Anthony, and I can't get them back. But I could have a future with the twins. If you'll just let me."

She hated the note of pleading that had somehow slipped into her tone.

And Cutty Grant must not have liked it much, either, because she saw his jaw clench suddenly and his voice turned tight. "I'm really not the bastard your father thought I was. The kind of bastard who would keep you from knowing your nieces."

"I didn't—I *don't*—think you're that. I just know there have to be hard feelings—"

"Harder than you'll ever know. But I'm well aware of the fact that you were only a kid, that you didn't have anything to do with it."

"Then will you let me stay?"

Again he didn't answer readily, and she knew he wasn't eager to agree even if he did need the help.

But in the end she thought that he might have wanted to prove he wasn't a bad guy, that he wasn't punishing her for something she'd had nothing to do with, because he said, "I suppose we can give it a try."

Kira was so happy to hear his decision that she couldn't help grinning. "Shall I start right now?" she asked with a glance at the clutter all around them.

"It'll all wait for tomorrow."

In that case Kira thought it was probably better to get out of there before he changed his mind.

"Then if you'll tell me where I can find a hotel or a motel I'll get a room and be back first thing in the morning."

Again he let silence reign as he seemed to consider something before he answered.

"If you aren't particular about the ambience you can stay out back. Where Marla and I lived when we first got here."

"No, I don't care about the ambience. And it's probably better if I'm close by."

He didn't look convinced of that but he didn't rescind the offer.

"Do you have a suitcase somewhere?" he asked instead.

"Out in the rental car."

"Why don't you go get it and I'll show you the accommodations?"

Kira didn't waste any time complying. She hurried out to the car, retrieved her bag from the trunk and went back inside.

Cutty didn't get to his feet until she was there. Then he did, leading the way from the living room through an open archway into a kitchen that was a disaster all its own.

He held the back door open for her, and she stepped into the small yard ahead of him, coming face-to-face with what looked to have been a garage once upon a time.

"This whole place belonged to my uncle Paulie.

He converted the garage into an apartment for Marla and me, and added another garage to the side of the house later on.''

"So this is where you lived after you eloped?'' Kira asked as they crossed the few feet of lawn and Cutty opened that door for her, too.

"Until my uncle died and left it all to us. Then we moved into the house. It's been fixed up and refurnished. Ordinarily I rent it to students from the college. But since it's summer vacation it's empty.''

Cutty reached in and flipped a switch. Three lamps went on at once, illuminating an open space arranged as a studio apartment.

There were no walls, so only the furnishings determined what each area was used for. A double bed and an armoire delineated the bedroom. A small sofa and matching armchair, a coffee table and a television designated the living room. And some kitchen cupboards, a sink, a two-burner stove with a tiny oven, a refrigerator and a small table with two chairs made up the kitchen.

"That door alongside the armoire will put you into the bathroom,'' Cutty explained without going farther than the doorway. "There's a tub with a shower in it but the water heater is pretty small so if you do a lot of dishes you'll want to wait half an hour before you take a bath.''

"I'm sure it'll be fine.''

What she *wasn't* sure of was why he had that dubious look on his face again, as if he was having second thoughts about this whole arrangement.

But if he was, he didn't say it.

Instead he said, "The girls are usually awake by seven."

"Seven. I'll be over before that," Kira said enthusiastically.

Cutty nodded his head. "There are towels in the bathroom. Sheets in the armoire. If you need anything before the morning—"

"I'll be fine."

He nodded again, which bothered Kira. If he didn't want to go ahead with this, why didn't he say something?

But all he said was, "Good night, then."

"See you first thing in the morning," Kira assured, moving to the door to see him out.

He turned to go without another word, leaving her with a view of his backside.

And although, as a rule, men's rear ends were not something she took notice of, it only required one glance to recognize that his was a great one.

A great rear end to go with the rest of his great body and his great face and his great hair.

Not that any of that mattered, because it didn't, she was quick to tell herself. She was only staying there for the babies, and anything about Cutty Grant was purely incidental.

Except that, incidental or not, she went on taking notice until Cutty Grant disappeared inside his house.

Chapter Two

Cutty had a hell of a time falling asleep Wednesday night and when he woke up before dawn Thursday morning it was aggravating to find his mind instantly on the mental treadmill that had kept him from sleeping in the first place. The treadmill Kira Wentworth's appearance on his doorstep had caused.

She'd really shaken things up for him, and as he rolled onto his back and tried to fall asleep again, he didn't feel any more sure of his decision to let her stick around.

He'd never expected to see any Wentworth again. Not after so many years and not when he was persona non grata in the extreme with Tom Wentworth.

Tom Wentworth who was the only Wentworth he ever really thought about when he thought about the family Marla had been estranged from. But then her adopted mother and adopted sister were just specks in the shadow Tom Wentworth cast, so it wasn't surprising that they wouldn't be uppermost on his mind for the last thirteen years.

Cutty opened his eyes and looked at the clock on his nightstand.

It was just after 5 a.m.

He doubted he would be able to sleep anymore but he didn't want to get up, either, so he cupped his hands under his head and stared at the ceiling.

He still couldn't believe that Kira Wentworth had shown up.

Marla's sister.

He'd only seen her once before. Actually, he'd only met her mother and father one time, too. But while Tom Wentworth's face was one Cutty would never forget, he had barely glanced at Kira before her adoptive father had ordered her to her room that night thirteen years ago. So there was no way Cutty had recognized her. If he had he might not have been so willing to let her come into his home. Her or anyone connected to Tom Wentworth.

Tom Wentworth.

Yeah, meeting him just once had been enough. More than enough, Cutty thought.

Marla's father hadn't wanted Marla to date in high school so she'd only seen Cutty on the sly. They'd made arrangements through friends; they'd met at the movies or the shopping mall; they'd seen each other at school functions. And always they'd had to keep an eye out for anyone who might report back to the controlling father, who ran his household with an iron fist.

But six months into dating, Marla had realized she was pregnant.

Cutty didn't think he'd ever seen anyone as afraid of anything as she'd been to tell her father.

Two seventeen-year-olds facing a nearly three-hundred-pound mountain of mean—the memory was still fresh in Cutty's mind.

To say it had been an ugly scene was an understatement. Tom Wentworth hadn't even wanted Cutty in the house. He'd hit the ceiling at just the sight of a boy there with his daughter. But Marla had insisted that they all needed to talk. Then she'd told her father what they'd come to tell him.

And all hell had broken loose.

Cutty still couldn't believe the way Tom Wentworth had exploded. It was as if a bomb had gone off in that living room. He'd screamed that Marla was a whore. A tramp. A good-for-nothing slut. And worse.

There hadn't been much Cutty could do during the tirade. Nothing much anyone could do but sit under the rain of hurtful, hateful words. But when Tom Wentworth had begun to demand that Marla have an abortion, Cutty had stood up to him. He'd told Tom Wentworth that Marla didn't want to have an abortion.

And Tom Wentworth had nearly beaten him to a pulp.

A few good punches of his own had saved Cutty,

but after that he'd been afraid to leave Marla there alone with her enraged bull of a father. So Cutty had taken Marla with him and left, not having any idea what he was going to do with her.

And a baby.

The sun began to make its rosy entrance through Cutty's bedroom curtains, and for a while he watched it, trying not to relive those early emotions that could still creep up on him every now and then. He'd been just a kid himself. A scared kid. With no one close by to turn to. He'd felt responsible. Overwhelmed. Terrified. He hadn't known what the hell he was going to do....

Lying there wasn't getting him anywhere, he decided suddenly and swung his legs over the side of the bed. He sat up on the edge, gripping the mattress and let his head drop forward.

Tom Wentworth had washed his hands of Marla—that's what he'd told her when she'd tried to call him the next day in hopes that he might have cooled off. She was on her own. He didn't care what happened to her.

Her adoptive mother had packed some of her clothes and sneaked them out to her because her father had said she wasn't even entitled to those.

And that had been that.

At least for a couple of years until Marla had gone behind Cutty's back. But that had been that in terms of Cutty and the Wentworths.

Until now.

Now when Kira Wentworth had shown up on his doorstep.

He really had thought she was the journalism student when he'd first caught sight of her coming up his porch steps. The journalism student had already interviewed his friend Ad, and Ad had told him she was slightly older than the average college student. That she was thin. Pretty. Blond.

Kira Wentworth fit that description. Although the minute he'd laid eyes on her he'd thought that he wouldn't say she was merely pretty. Kira Wentworth was beautiful. And her hair wasn't just blond. It was the color of honey shot through with sunlight. Plus she had skin like alabaster. And the softest mouth he'd ever seen. And a small, streamlined nose. And those eyes! They were the blue of a summer sky on a cloudless day. Not to mention that for a petite woman she had a body that wouldn't quit....

So, okay, he couldn't deny that that first sight of her had stirred things inside him that hadn't been stirred for a long, long time. But how confusing was it that the first person he'd been attracted to, since he seemed to have gotten his head together again after Marla's and Anthony's deaths, was a Wentworth?

Incredibly confusing, that's how confusing it was.

Rationally, Cutty knew there was no reason to hold a grudge against Kira Wentworth. But that had been his reaction when she'd told him who she was. In spite of his initial attraction to her. He'd been tempted to kick her out of his house. What had gone through his mind was that he didn't want any Wentworth anywhere near him because with any Wentworth came the potential for contact with Tom Wentworth. Or the effects of having been raised by him.

But Cutty hadn't wanted to be a hard-ass, so he'd tried to curb the feelings.

And apparently he'd been pretty successful, since only a few minutes later his heart had gone out to Kira when he'd told her about Marla and Anthony and witnessed the blow that struck.

He'd been so successful at curbing his negative feelings that he'd even been tempted to comfort her with a hug.

Well, more than a hug. What he'd really been inclined to do was take her in his arms, learn what it would feel like to have her head pressed to his chest, her body against his....

But she's a Wentworth, he'd reminded himself to chase away that urge.

Or at least to resist it. The urge hadn't exactly gone away, he just hadn't acted on it.

In fact, he'd still been struggling with it when she'd offered to come in and care for the twins. And him.

He hadn't expected that and once more his emotions had taken a swing toward the negative. He'd instantly imagined another Wentworth in his house. He'd flashed on the way things had been. On the way they could be again.

Cutty closed his eyes and shook his head as if that would get rid of the thoughts that he felt guilty for having had the night before and again now. Thoughts of Marla. Of life with Marla.

But guilty or not, the bottom line had been he really hadn't been thrilled with the prospect of Kira stepping in for Betty.

After all, she'd been raised by the same man Marla had. And there she'd been, with the ink barely dry on her Ph.D. as a clue to the likelihood that she was an overachiever, not a hair out of place, not a wrinkle in her clothes, her makeup flawless, her posture perfect, and Cutty hadn't had a doubt she was cut from the same cloth Marla was.

So no, he hadn't wanted Kira's help.

Only she'd made him feel like a heel for denying, not only the help she was offering, but for denying her the chance to meet the twins. To get to know them. To be a part of their lives.

They were her nieces, after all, and Cutty had known that if Marla had been there she would have welcomed Kira with open arms—both for herself and for the girls. He'd known that Marla would have wanted her younger sister to know her daughters.

So he'd caved.

Cutty opened his eyes and sighed, disgusted with himself. Just when he'd thought his life was finally settling down, here he was in a muddle of conflicting thoughts, conflicting feelings again. And for about the tenth time, he asked himself if he'd really accepted her help as temporary nanny and housekeeper because it was what Marla would have wanted, or if he'd had some kind of attraction to her. In spite of himself.

He hoped he'd only accepted her help because it was what Marla would have wanted.

Sure he'd told Ad a couple of weeks ago that he thought he was finally ready to get back into the swing of things again. But slowly. Cautiously. With great care and consideration given to exactly who— and what—he let into his life again.

And a pair of blue eyes—no matter how incredible a blue they were—didn't change that.

He grabbed his cane from where it rested against the nightstand and got to his feet.

Kira would do the same job Betty did, and he would make sure his relationship with her was no different than the relationship he had with Betty— purely friendly.

And that was all there was to it.

Because while he might have finally made it over the hump of grief and been ready to restart his life, it wouldn't be with Kira Wentworth.

What he was ready for was an ordinary, everyday woman who took things in stride, who knew when to put on the full-court press and when not to, who knew the value of people over the value of appearances, who stopped long enough to smell the flowers.

And he didn't think for a minute that Dr. Over- achiever Microbiologist Kira Wentworth was that woman.

After a restless night, Kira was awake before her alarm went off. The moment she remembered where she was and what she was slated to do today, she was too antsy to linger in bed. She got up and went into the bathroom for a quick shower.

The sun was just dawning when she came out of the bathroom and stood in front of the armoire to survey the clothes she'd brought with her. She didn't have the slightest idea what was involved in taking care of eighteen-month-old babies, which meant she wasn't sure what to wear. But she was sure that she wanted it to be just right.

Not that she thought her nieces would even notice what she had on, but she so desperately wanted them to like her that every detail of this first meeting seemed important.

Maybe something bright, she thought, taking out a red silk shirt.

Or was that *too* bright? Would it scare them?

Maybe.

She replaced the shirt in the armoire and continued the search.

Definitely not the black high-necked blouse, she decided when that was the next thing that caught her eye. Black was too austere. It might send the message that she wasn't accessible and the last thing she wanted was for her nieces to see her as standoffish.

And white might make her look too washed out, so she decided against the white rayon cap shirt, too.

Kira was tempted to wear the flowered sundress with the full skirt but she wasn't sure if that was practical. Although she did give it a second look when it also occurred to her that this was essentially her first day on a new job and making a good impression was probably not a bad idea.

But the impression she was thinking of making

with the dress was on Cutty and the moment she realized that was what was dancing on the edges of her mind she shied away from the sundress for sure.

She wasn't in Northbridge to impress Cutty. Her goal was connecting with the babies—*only* with the babies—and she wouldn't let herself be distracted from that. Not even by a pair of deep, dark green eyes that had longer, thicker lashes than any man should be entitled to.

No, she wasn't even going to think about him. Wasn't that what she'd told herself the night before when she'd had so much trouble getting to sleep because every time she'd closed her eyes he was there, in her thoughts? There was one reason and only one reason she'd come to Montana and that was to try to have what remained of her family in her life again. And what remained of her family were the twins. Cutty was merely incidental. To her at least. He was just the person she had to go through to get to her nieces.

So what was she going to wear? she asked herself.

She forced herself to focus on the clothes in the armoire. To concentrate.

What about the linen slacks and the short-sleeved yellow silk blouse with the banded collar?

Comfortable but not sloppy. A little color but not too much. Sort of casual—because Cutty had made that odd comment about how he liked things casual—whatever that meant. So, okay, the linen slacks and the yellow blouse it was, she decided.

The slacks that made her rear end look good.

Not that that was a factor in her choosing them, she swore to herself. It was just a coincidence.

She took the pants and the shirt to the bed and laid them out before she turned to the small dressing table to do her hair and makeup.

Although she would ordinarily have worn her hair loose on the first day of a new job, for this particular job she thought it should probably be kept under control. That meant pulling it away from her face. A French knot seemed too stiff and formal, but she thought that a ponytail might be just the ticket. So she brushed her hair, pulling it tightly back and tying a pale yellow scarf around it to keep it there.

Once she was finished with her hair she applied a little blush, mascara and lipstick. Then she returned to the bed to put on the clothes she'd chosen before pulling on trouser socks and loafers, and concluding that she was ready to face the day and this new undertaking.

Ready and eager.

"To meet the twins," she said out loud, as if someone had accused her of being eager for more than meeting her nieces.

And that wasn't the case. She wasn't eager to see Cutty again, she tried to convince herself. How could she be eager to see the person who would no doubt be watching her every move, judging her, comparing her to Marla?

Of course she wasn't looking forward to that. Even if the person doing the judging *had* turned into a staggeringly handsome man.

Aunt Kira, I'm just here to be Aunt Kira.

Aunt Kira.

And Marla had been Mom…

That seemed so strange.

Whenever Kira thought of her sister she thought of the age Marla had been the last time Kira had seen her—seventeen. Just a teenager.

But Marla had grown up. She'd been a wife. A mother.

And now she wasn't just out in the world somewhere where Kira had hope of finding her again. Now she was lost to Kira forever. Tears flooded her eyes. Tears for her lost sister, for her lost nephew.

Kira knew there was nothing she could do to bring back either of them and reminded herself that there were still the twins. Marla's twins. And if she couldn't have Marla, if she couldn't ever know Anthony, at least she could maintain her connection with her sister through those babies.

Which was exactly what she intended to do, she vowed as she left the dressing table to make the bed, fighting the longing that things had been different. That her family hadn't ended up the way it had.

And not just because it would have been nice to have had Marla and Anthony in her life. If things had been different and Marla hadn't been estranged from them all it might have also been easier for Kira to think of Cutty Grant as her sister's husband, as someone who was off-limits.

As it was, she didn't have any sense of him as family. Maybe that was part of why it was so difficult to get past how attractive he was. So difficult not to notice it. Not to be affected by it the way any woman would be affected by it.

She was determined not to be, though, Kira told herself forcefully. She was going to have with the twins what she'd missed with Anthony. To be Aunt Kira now, even if she hadn't been before.

Aunt Kira, she thought, moving into the tiny bathroom to straighten it. *Nothing but Aunt Kira.*

And she meant it, too.

It was just that it would have been so much easier just to be Aunt Kira if Cutty wasn't going to be right there with her every minute. Right there where all she would have to do was look up to see his face. Those eyes. That big, hard body...

But she wasn't going to let herself be affected by it. She wasn't. She really wasn't.

She was going to do the best she could to take care of the twins, to get to know them, to earn their love, and in the process she was also going to keep their father nothing more than a sidebar to her relationship with them.

She was going to make sure of that if it was the last thing she ever did.

It was just that it might not only be the *last* thing she ever did.

It also might be the hardest...

Kira left the apartment at 6:45.

As she crossed the yard she wondered if Cutty would be awake yet or if he stayed in bed until the twins woke him. If that was the case and she couldn't get into the house, she had every intention of waiting outside the back door on one of the patio chairs just to make sure that she was there the minute she was needed.

But when she got to the house the back door was open and through the screen she could smell bacon frying and see Cutty sitting at the kitchen table—his foot propped on a second kitchen chair. There were also two babies in matching high chairs on the other side of the table, and a short, plump, older woman who was setting bowls on the high chairs' trays.

Kira felt a sinking feeling at the thought that she was already late. That someone else had had to come in to do the job she'd volunteered for.

But she didn't want to make it any worse by wasting time standing there looking in from outside, so she knocked on the screen door's frame.

Cutty looked away from the twins and that first glance of those evergreen eyes sent the oddest sensation through Kira. It was like a tiny jolt that skittered across the surface of her skin.

"Come on in," Cutty encouraged.

Kira opened the screen and went in, apologizing as she did. "I'm sorry if I'm late. I thought you said seven was early enough to get here and it's not even that yet."

"I did say seven was early enough," Cutty responded. "But Betty—this is Betty Cunningham," he interrupted himself to do the introductions. "Betty, this is Kira, Marla's sister. Anyway, Betty came over early on her way to the hospital to get her mother, and I dropped the cane coming down the stairs and woke the girls, so here we are.''

Betty had waited for him to finish, but just barely before she came to stand directly in front of Kira to wrap her arms around her and give her an unexpected hug. "It's so nice to meet our Marla's sister.''

Kira tried not to stiffen up at the physical contact from the stranger. "Thank you,'' she said. "It's nice to meet you, too.''

Betty released her and turned toward the table, extending one hand in the direction of the twins as if they were the prize on a game show. "And these are our darlings. Cutty said you didn't get to see them last night.''

And that was when Kira got her first real look at her nieces.

She'd never been an easy crier before, and she didn't know what was wrong with her now, but yet again quick tears filled her eyes at that initial glimpse of the two babies, who were paying no attention to her whatsoever.

There wasn't any question that they were Cutty's children but there was enough of Marla in them to cause Kira's tears. Identical, they both had Cutty's sable-colored hair in tight caps of curls that were just like Marla's. They had big green eyes slightly lighter than Cutty's, chubby cheeks and rosebud mouths like Marla, and the cutest turned-up noses Kira thought she'd ever seen.

"This is Mandy,'' Cutty said, pointing to the baby

on the right. "And this is Mel—short for Melanie. About the only way any of us can tell them apart is that Mel has that tiny mole above her left eye. We're hoping Mandy doesn't get one like it or we'll have to go back to guessing which of them is which."

Fighting the tears because she was afraid Cutty and Betty would think she was crazy if they saw them and because she didn't want to alarm the babies, Kira went to the table and leaned across it.

"Hi, Mandy. Hi, Mel."

They were doing more playing with their oatmeal than eating it—Mel had a handful she was squishing through her fingers and Mandy was taking spoonfuls and placing them meticulously on the tray around the bowl—but they finally looked up from what they were doing.

Kira didn't know what she'd expected, but it wasn't what she got. Mel immediately held out her arms to Betty as if to save her from Kira, and Mandy's adorable little face screwed up into a look of great alarm before she let out a wail.

That made Kira *really* want to cry.

"Oh, no, it's all right. I'm your aunt," she said as if that would make any difference.

It didn't.

Betty hurried to the high chairs, standing behind them and wrapping a comforting arm around each of the babies as she bent over between them to pull their cheeks to hers.

"Poor little dears," she cooed to them. "They're usually so good with strangers."

"It's okay, girls," Cutty assured his daughters. "Kira's a nice lady."

Mandy had cut short her wail, but both babies still stared at Kira as if she were some kind of alien life-form.

"Just give them a little time. They'll warm up to you," Betty said.

"Sure they will," Cutty chimed in.

It didn't make Kira feel any better.

And it wasn't much help when Cutty said, "Betty, why don't you show Kira the ropes around here so the girls will eat?"

Kira didn't think it was a good sign that she had to be removed from her nieces' sight in order for them to relax enough to have their breakfast. But there was nothing she could do except comply and hope the twins would warm up to her. Eventually.

Disheartened, Kira followed Betty out of the kitchen.

"Really, they'll be okay after a while," the older woman said confidently.

"I hope you're right."

That seemed to put an end to the subject then, because Betty said, "Let's start in the nursery," and led Kira down the hallway that ran alongside the staircase and up the steps.

The second floor of the house was as much of a disaster as the first. On the way to the nursery Betty picked up a few things, but it didn't make a dent in the mess.

The nursery itself was painted white and trimmed

in mauve, with one wall papered in a print where cartoonish jungle animals all played happily in a rain forest.

There were two cribs, two dressers, two toy boxes, but only one changing table.

"That's Mel's bed. That's Mandy's," Betty began, pointing out which was which. "But sometimes if one or the other of the girls is fussy they sleep better if you put them in the same crib."

The older woman crossed to Mandy's bed and began to strip off the sheet. "I probably have enough time to help you with these beds. Marla always changed the bedding every day. I've tried to go on doing things like she did because I know that's what she would have wanted."

There was a strong message implied that Kira should do things as Marla would have wanted, too.

Kira went to the other crib and began to strip the sheet from it. "You must have known Marla well."

"Northbridge is a small town—everyone knows everyone well. And then I helped out three days a week after the twins were born so I got to know her even better. Not that Marla really needed any help, because believe you me, she didn't. It was Cutty who brought me in but I mostly just fed the babies bottles and tried to play with Anthony while Marla did the real work. She was just a marvel as a mother and housekeeper. Actually I can't think of anything she wasn't a marvel at."

Unlike her younger sister, Kira thought, as she lost her grip on the crib sheet three times before she finally succeeded in getting it stretched over all four corners of the mattress.

But at least the other woman didn't notice. Betty just continued talking. "You should have seen Marla with Anthony. He was a sweet boy but he was a handful. It never fazed your sister, though. She was devoted to him. She was like a saint, that girl."

Kira didn't know what to say to that, especially since what Betty was saying was making Kira worry about how she was going to accomplish all Marla apparently had.

Betty then hurried out of the room with the sheets in her arms, saying as she did, "You can do the rest of the room later. In the meantime we can put these sheets right into the washer. Marla always did at least one load of laundry a day, and I'm sure you'll want to, too."

Kira watched the plump older lady stuff the sheets into the washing machine in the closetlike space that opened off the hall, hoping it and the dryer operated the same way the machines in her apartment laundry room did so she wouldn't have to ask for instructions.

"Cutty told me this morning that he's not having you do anything in his room. He says he'll take care of it himself," Betty informed her, bypassing the closed door across the hall from the nursery and moving into the bathroom where towels, washcloths, baby clothes, tub toys and various soaps, shampoos and lotions littered the space. There was also a ring around the tub and stains all over the sink and countertop.

"Baths everyday," Betty instructed. "In the evenings before bed. That was how Marla did it. And she would never have left the bathtub dirty. Or a speck of dust anywhere or the floors unvacuumed or—well, or anything less than immaculate. I'm telling you, she was amazing."

"She always was," Kira said, trying to do a little in the way of straightening up the bathroom.

"Oh, honey, no. Marla kept that soap dispenser on the right side of the sink and that's where it belongs."

Kira put the pump bottle where she'd been told to.

Betty adjusted it to just the right spot, explaining as she did, "Marla liked everything exactly so. But I don't have much time, and you can get this done later. Let's go back downstairs so I can show you a few things there."

The older woman led the way out of the bathroom and Kira followed.

There was another closed door on the other side of the bathroom and Betty nodded in that direction as they went by it.

"That was Anthony's room," she whispered as if it were a secret. "There's nothing in there. Even when Anthony was here he could only have a mattress on the floor, and at the start of the summer Cutty finally got rid of it. He gave away his own bed and bedroom furniture, too. It was a clean sweep. He bought all new things for himself, but of course there was no reason to get anything for Anthony's old room. Besides, there's work that needs to be done in there and until it is... Well, no sense furnishing it."

Kira glanced in the direction of the closed door, curious about what kind of work the room needed and why. But she didn't feel comfortable asking so she merely followed Betty down the stairs as the woman continued her nonstop chatter.

"It was good for Cutty to make some changes, though. We all thought it meant he was ready to get on with his life, and we were glad to see it. For his sake and for Mandy's and Mel's. A person can't grieve forever. That's just not healthy. Would you look at this mess?" Betty said, changing subjects as they reached the living room but not taking so much as a breath to let Kira know she was suddenly talking about something else. "Two days I've been gone, and I just can't believe what a shambles this place is in. You came at the right time, that's for sure. Now I can take care of my mother and know everything here will be all right. If poor Marla saw a mess like this she'd have had a fit. Never a thing out of order—that was Marla."

Betty went on to point out the box in the corner of the room where the downstairs toys could be put away, as well as outlining how often Marla had washed windows. And turned mattresses. And scrubbed walls. And wiped down baseboards. And polished furniture and silver. And made hot meals and home-baked cakes and cookies and her own bread.

The list seemed to go on and on until Kira began to think she might have a panic attack if she heard one more word.

Maybe Betty saw it on her face because she

stopped suddenly and said, "Oh, not that you have to do all Marla did. I don't know if anyone could do all Marla did. I'll just be happy if you can keep everybody clean and fed and the house picked up until I can get back here."

"I'll do my best," Kira said, realizing that Marla had left her a very high standard to live up to.

"I'm sure you'll be fine," Betty said. "Now let me give you a quick tour of the kitchen and tell you about the babies' schedule before I let you get to work."

Kira followed the plump woman back to the kitchen where Cutty was trying to coax his daughters to eat.

The reappearance of Kira didn't aid that cause because this time when she walked into the room they watched her warily and paid no attention to what their father wanted of them.

"After breakfast I get the darlings cleaned up and dressed for the day," Betty was saying, oblivious to the twins' continuing disenchantment with Kira. "Some mornings they'll watch *Sesame Street* while I get to work on the house, or they'll play—"

"Those are the good mornings," Cutty contributed wryly, leaving Kira to guess what happened on the bad mornings.

Betty didn't address it, though, she just went on. "They're ready for lunch around noon and then I let them digest their food for about half an hour before I put them down for their naps. That's the best time to catch up. They'll be awake again about three or so. We try to have dinner around six. Then there are baths and hair washing. They like to look at books before bedtime—they won't sit still if you try to read to them but if you point to the pictures and tell them what they are, they like that. I put them to bed for the night about eight or eight-thirty, and that's the day.''

Kira felt winded just listening to it.

But she wasn't going to let either Betty or Cutty know that and decided she would look at it all as a challenge. A challenge she was confident she could meet just the way she'd always met every other challenge in her life. After all, she'd been well-trained in meeting standards set by someone else. Plus she kept her own apartment pristinely clean. How much more difficult could it be to take care of two little girls on top of doing the housework around here?

''Okay,'' she said simply enough.

''You'll do fine,'' Betty insisted, looking at her watch. ''I'd better leave you to it so I can get Mom out of that hospital before she tries hitchhiking home. She warned me to be there first thing this morning or else. But if you all need me—''

''Don't worry about us. We'll manage,'' Cutty said.

''What's this *we* business?'' Betty countered. ''Remember, you're supposed to stay off that ankle. You just let Kira do everything. After all, she's Marla's sister. She'll be able to handle anything.''

Kira didn't refute that because she knew she would bend over backward to do every bit as well as Marla had. As always.

"Okay, I'm off," Betty announced.

She kissed the babies on the top of their curly heads as Cutty said, "Tell your Mom hi and that we hope she feels better."

"I will," Betty answered before bustling out amidst her goodbyes.

And then there Kira was, alone with Cutty and that incredible face that looked amused at something, and two babies who both eyed her warily.

"Are you sure you're up for this?" Cutty asked then.

"Absolutely," she said.

And she honestly thought she was.

Even as she glanced around at the stacks of dirty dishes, at the babies who seemed to hate her, and thought about all she suddenly found herself in charge of.

Marla had done it. And done it well.

She would, too.

"You were on your ankle too much, weren't you?"

It was nine o'clock that night before Cutty got the twins to bed and, coming down the stairs after putting laundry in the dryer, Kira saw him flinch as he sat on the couch and raised his foot onto the throw pillow on the coffee table.

"It's okay," he said, looking embarrassed to have been caught showing pain.

But it was Kira who was really embarrassed. She'd been much more hindrance than help today and she knew it. She had only to look around at the chaos that had grown rather than diminished to realize just what a detriment she'd been.

"Why don't you sit down so we can talk?" Cutty said then.

"That sounds bad. You're going to fire me, aren't you?"

He laughed. A deep rumble of a laugh that sounded better than it should have to Kira. "You just look like you need to sit down," he said.

She caught sight of her reflection in the living room's picture window and was nearly startled by what she saw. Her blouse was partially hanging out of the waistband of slacks stained with Mandy's chicken-noodle soup from lunch, half of her hair had slipped from the scarf-tied ponytail and the other half was bulging out of it more on one side of her head than the other, and all in all she looked as if she'd just been through the wringer. In fact, she was more of a wreck than the house was.

"Oh," she said, reaching up to snatch the yellow scarf so her hair could fall free. She stuffed the scarf into her pocket and then finger-combed her hair into some sort of order.

"Come on. Sit a minute," Cutty urged.

She did, perching like a schoolgirl on the edge of the easy chair to his left.

Cutty's dark green eyes studied her, and it occurred to Kira that even though they'd basically been together all day and evening she'd been so enmeshed in one thing after another that she'd hardly glanced at him.

He didn't look any the worse for wear, though. The gray workout pants that stretched across his massive thighs and the muscle-hugging white T-shirt he wore were still clean. Even the five o'clock shadow that darkened the lower half of his striking face only gave him a scruffiness that was very sexy.

But the last thing Kira needed was to notice *that* now.

To avoid it she forced herself to stare at the applesauce caked on her shoe. "I'm so sorry about…" She shrugged helplessly. "Everything today. Really, I swear I'm usually the most organized, efficient person anyone knows. And believe it or not, my apartment is always spotless."

"I don't doubt it," he said. "But add a couple of busy, mischievous eighteen-month-olds to the equation and it tends to throw everything off."

Why did he seem to think her failure today was funny?

"Even when my focus was on school and I was under a lot of pressure to get grades as high as Marla always had, I could still juggle all my work at home with all my classwork and even my research. My room at home and my apartment after I left home never looked like this…" Kira motioned to the even bigger mess all around them. "I was sure if Marla was a whiz at all of it the way Betty said she was, that I would be, too."

"Marla wasn't *always* a whiz at it. She started out having trouble taking care of a baby—*one* baby—and everything else, too. We both did. But as time went on—"

"I'll get better," Kira promised before he could finish what he was saying. "I mean it. I'll come over here at four tomorrow morning before you or the girls are awake and—"

"Whoa!" Cutty said with a shake of his head and a big hand held up palm outward. "I didn't want to talk to you about trying harder—"

"So you *are* firing me."

"I never hired you, how could I fire you? You're just helping out and all I wanted to talk to you about was relaxing."

"Relaxing?" Kira repeated as if the word wasn't in her vocabulary.

"I think you're trying too hard and getting in your own way."

Trying too hard? Was there such a thing?

"It's making you kind of fumble fingered."

"I know I seemed to drop and spill everything I touched today, and I spent all my time cleaning up my own messes rather than making any headway with the ones that were already here. I'm not usually that clumsy."

"And when it comes to the girls—"

"They still don't like me."

"You're just unfamiliar to them, and they're missing Betty—she's like a grandmother to them. They'll get used to you but you can't force it. They can be pretty contrary when you try."

And Kira had the soiled clothes and shoes to show for it.

Still she knew he was right. The way she'd handled the twins certainly hadn't been the recipe for success, since all they'd wanted to do was escape from her overly cloying attentions—frequently by displays of temper—and Cutty had ended up having to step in to do everything.

"I'm sorry," Kira said again. Then, with another glance at the debris all around them, she added, "Maybe I can get some things done now."

"I think what you should do now is go soak in a bubble bath," Cutty said. "And we'll start over tomorrow. Maybe *without* so much concern about how Marla did things."

Kira had spent an inordinate amount of time asking how her sister did everything. "Betty said—"

"I can imagine what Betty said. But Betty isn't here and neither is Marla, and we just need to get things taken care of regardless of what Betty said or how Marla did things."

"Okay," Kira agreed, thinking that that was a nice way of saying she just needed to get *something—anything*—done.

But then he managed to raise her sinking spirits with a simple, winning smile. "You know, I appreciate that you're here and willing to help out. And I'm glad you want to get to know the girls. I just think things will run more smoothly if you can go with the flow. Like I said, *relax*. Have a little fun, get a little done. There's no right way. There's no wrong way. There's no big deals.''

Kira nodded. ''I'll try.'' But the truth was, she'd been taught that there was *always* a right way and that was how she had to do everything. She wasn't too sure she could ignore that now.

Cutty took his foot off the pillow and stood then. ''Come on. Let me give you a key to the back door so you can get in whenever you want, and then you can go have that long soak in the tub. Tomorrow will be a better day.''

Kira thought he was probably figuring it couldn't be a worse one.

But still, the idea of sinking into a bath full of bubbles was too tempting to pass up and she stood, too, following Cutty to the kitchen and feeling guilty for the sight of him limping even more than he had been the night before.

''I really am sorry,'' she told him yet again as they reached the kitchen.

''I'll let it go this time but another day like today and I'll have to dock your pay,'' he joked.

He took a key from the hook beside the door and turned around, giving her a full view of a mischievous smile that put those creases on either side of his mouth and made an unexpected warmth wash through her.

''Before this is over I might end up having to pay you,'' Kira said, making a joke of her own. ''In fact you can probably start a tab with those two dishes and the coffee mug I broke.''

Cutty just laughed and again she liked the sound of it. "You are kind of a bull in a china shop," he said as if it were a compliment.

"Not usually," she assured. "Honestly, no one who knows me would have believed this today."

He didn't say anything to that. He merely gave her the key.

But as she accepted it their hands brushed. Only briefly. And Kira found herself oddly aware of it. Of the heat of his skin. Of the little shards of electricity that seemed to shoot up her arm from the point of contact.

It was just silly, she told herself.

Although, she also thought when Cutty spoke again that his voice might have dropped an octave, and she had to wonder if he'd felt it, too.

But if he did, he didn't indicate it in *what* he was saying.

"And don't even think about coming over here at four tomorrow morning. Seven is plenty early enough. You'll probably have to wait half an hour or so for the girls to wake up even at that. But maybe if you're the first person they see instead of Betty, it'll start things off more in your favor."

"Like ducks bonding to the first thing they see when they hatch?"

He grinned. "Something like that, yeah."

"I'll hope for the best."

There was a moment then when their eyes met and held. Kira didn't understand why or what was in the air between them when it happened. But there was definitely *something* in the air between them. Something that seemed more than just the camaraderie of being in the trenches together.

But then it passed and Cutty opened the screen for her, holding it while she went out.

"See you in the morning," he said then.

"Good night," she responded.

But even as Kira walked across the yard to the garage apartment she could still feel the remnants of that change that had hung in the air for that single moment.

What had that been about? she wondered.

She honestly didn't know.

But she did know that even after the fact, it left her feeling all tingly inside.

Chapter Three

"It was the weirdest damn thing. There was this minute when I actually thought about *kissing* her."

Cutty was sitting in the kitchen of Ad Walker's apartment at seven-fifteen the next morning with his ankle propped on one of Ad's chairs.

Ad was Cutty's best friend and after Cutty had suggested to Kira that he leave her alone with the twins this morning, he'd done just that. His police-issue SUV had an automatic transmission, and since it didn't have a clutch and it was his left foot that was out of commission, he could drive even if he wasn't supposed to walk any more than necessary.

He'd taken advantage of that fact and driven to the restaurant-bar Ad owned on Main Street. There were two apartments above Adz, one in which Ad lived.

Cutty had had to hop on one foot to get up the outside stairs but once he had he'd pounded on Ad's apartment door until Ad woke up to let him in.

A bleary-eyed Ad had made coffee, and it was over two cups of that strong, black brew that Cutty had told him about the appearance of Kira Wentworth on his doorstep and her insistence on staying to help out.

Cutty had also told Ad what had been on his mind since Kira had walked through his door, culminating in that moment when he and Kira had been saying good-night the evening before and the air all around them had seemed charged.

"So you just *thought* about kissing her? You didn't do it?" Ad asked, sitting across the table from Cutty in the same position—with his legs propped on the remaining chair even though they weren't in need of elevation.

"No, I didn't do it," Cutty answered as if the question was ridiculous.

"I think you should have."

"Come on," Cutty said as if his friend had to be kidding.

"Why not? A beautiful woman shows up out of the blue—the first woman I've ever heard you say that about, by the way. You have trouble keeping your eyes off her all day long—especially when she's bending over," Ad said, summarizing what Cutty had already told him. "You felt sparks—even though you don't understand it. Who's to say she didn't feel them, too?"

"Come on," Cutty repeated, this time with a groan.

But Ad wasn't fazed. "You said yourself that it was time you got back on the horse—so to speak. I don't see anything wrong with going for it."

"She's Marla's *sister*," Cutty reminded.

"Well, sure, technically. But she's Marla's *adopted* sister. They weren't related by blood. Plus, they only shared a roof when they were kids and not even for their whole childhoods. If Marla were alive and they passed each other on the street they might not have even recognized each other. And no matter what their relationship was a lifetime ago, the bottom line is that to you, this woman is just a woman. No different than if she was a newcomer to Northbridge who you met at church."

"Still," Cutty persisted with his coffee cup poised at his lips so he could take a drink after the word left his mouth.

"Good argument," Ad countered sardonically. "And the reason you don't *have* a good argument is that this woman being Marla's *adopted* sister is absolutely no reason you couldn't have a thing with her."

"You have to admit it's a little—"

"It's a little nothing. I can't see where there would be a single thing wrong with it. Two separate women. Mostly unrelated to each other. It's not freaky so stop even thinking that it might be."

Cutty gave him a mock salute, pretending to take the order.

"There is a bigger issue here, though," Ad went on. "Is this Kira like Marla?"

There weren't many people who had known the real Marla. But Ad had. He was also the only person Cutty felt free to talk to honestly because he was the only person Cutty had ever confided in about his late wife and marriage.

"That's not just a bigger issue," Cutty said. "It's a huge issue."

"So she *is* like Marla?"

Cutty shrugged. "I don't know. Maybe. Maybe not. She was raised by Marla's father—that's not much of an endorsement. I don't think he would have let anybody get away with being less than a shining monument to him. She has a Ph.D. in microbiology—that can't mean she's a slacker. And since she didn't get enough done yesterday she was downstairs trying to clean the kitchen at six this morning even though I told her point-blank to come around seven when the girls usually wake up."

Ad's eyebrows rose. "Not good signs," he agreed.

"On the other hand," Cutty said, and he couldn't help laughing when he did, "she hit my place like a second tornado. So far she's been all thumbs. She's broken dishes. Spilled cereal. Made a mess of everything she's touched. And even though she swears she's usually a great housekeeper and it's just trying to keep up with the twins that's causing it, I may not find my house still standing when I get back."

"And you liked that she made mistakes," Ad accused.

"I wouldn't say I *liked* it. I need help around there, somebody to take Betty's place, and I'm sure as hell not getting that with Kira. I was on this ankle so much yesterday and last night that I had to take a pain pill to get the throbbing to quit so I could sleep. I haven't had to do that in three days.''

"Okay, so while it might indicate that she's different from Marla, it's not doing you much good right now," Ad amended. "How is she with the girls?"

"Oh, so bad. I'm liable to have to arrest myself for being a neglectful parent because I left them alone with her this morning."

"They'll be fine. They've survived my baby-sitting in a pinch."

"And Kira's about as bad at it as you are. Although it's also possible that the twins might hurt her," Cutty added with another laugh. "They don't like her yet, that's for sure. I'm hoping if she gets them up this morning and neither Betty or I are anywhere around, they'll have to let her take care of them and maybe that'll break some of the ice. But as it stands now, she is definitely not their favorite person."

"None of this makes her sound much like Marla," Ad observed.

Cutty sobered again and Ad caught it and said, "But something about her is like Marla. What?"

"She *wants* to do it all the way Marla did. She doesn't know how to accomplish it—yet—but I can tell that's how high she's set the bar."

Ad didn't have anything to say to that right away. Instead he took a drink of his coffee and then stared at the cup even after he'd set it back on the table.

"I can't get into that...that whole perfection thing

again, you know?'' Cutty said then, his voice quiet, solemn, determined. And reluctant, too. Reluctant to even allude to anything that spoke badly of his late wife.

"Yeah," Ad agreed the same way.

"I'm not even going to take the chance."

"So you didn't kiss her."

Cutty shook his head.

"But you wanted to," Ad said on a more upbeat note. "At least that means you really are back in the land of the living."

"Or that I'm just a glutton for punishment," Cutty countered wryly.

"That, too," Ad confirmed with a laugh. Then he said, "Maybe I should come by and meet her. Give you my expert opinion."

"You just want to check her out."

"That, too," Ad repeated with another laugh.

"Okay. But you'd better be on your best behavior."

"Nothing less."

"Any chance you could make it over tonight? When I saw how things were going yesterday I had to call that journalism student and reschedule my half of the interview for tonight. Only tonight she has to be there at seven, which means the twins will still be up. Maybe you could help Kira keep the girls out of the way while I talk to the reporter."

"Sure."

"Great. And will you do me a favor? Will you run

by my office later today when your brother starts his shift and get that paperwork from him?''

One of Ad's brothers was Cutty's partner on Northbridge's police force.

"You're supposed to be recuperating, not working," Ad reminded.

"Paperwork doesn't put any weight on my ankle, and at least I'll feel like I'm doing something to earn my paycheck."

"Uh-huh. And I guess it's a good idea to have something to keep you from watching your new housekeeper bending over."

"Oh, yeah," Cutty agreed.

The problem was, he doubted that paperwork would do the trick any more than anything he'd tried the day before.

There was just something about Kira that had his eyes wandering to her like heat-seeking missiles every time she was in sight.

Whether she was bending over or not.

Kira felt as if she were walking to the guillotine as she climbed the stairs at 7:45 that morning. She was on her own. Cutty was gone. There was no chance of Betty bustling in to rescue her. And one of the twins was calling, "Da...Da..." from the nursery.

It was a cute, pleasant little summons of Cutty. Kira hoped that meant that at least one of the girls was in a more receptive mood than yesterday. But even if one or both of the twins was happy now, that didn't necessarily mean the high spirits would last when Kira showed her face in the room.

"Just be positive and upbeat," she advised herself as she reached the nursery door. "Positive and upbeat and don't try too hard," she added, recalling what Cutty had said the night before.

She closed her eyes and willed the tension out of her shoulders. But it didn't help much and when the next, "Da!" was more insistent, she decided keeping the twins waiting too long was not going to get the day started on the right foot, either.

So she opened her eyes and the nursery door and went in.

"Good morning," she said cheerily. Probably too cheerily.

Mel and Mandy were both standing up in their respective cribs, grasping the railings for balance. Cutty had told her that in the summer heat he let them sleep in only their diapers. But Mel had taken off even that. And neither of them was glad to see Kira.

"Da?" Mel queried, her tiny forehead wrinkled into a frown that threatened tears.

"Your daddy isn't home this morning. He's at work," Kira lied, hoping their daddy being at work was something that registered as routine for them.

Maybe she was right because although Mel's bottom lip came out in an elaborate pout, she didn't cry.

"Down," Mandy demanded then.

"We have to get a diaper on Mel before she has an accident," Kira answered.

"Down!" Mandy insisted.

Wanting to please her, Kira went to Mandy's crib. "Okay, I'll put you down to play with your toys while I get a diaper on Mel. Then it's your turn."

Kira lifted Mandy out of her crib and set her on the floor before picking up Mel and taking her to the changing table.

Within moments of setting Mel on the changing table, Mandy toddled out of the nursery.

"No! Mandy, come back here!"

Mandy didn't so much as pause in her flight.

But there was Mel, already on the changing table, stark naked, and Kira couldn't leave her.

"Let's do this fast," she muttered to herself, reaching for a fresh disposable diaper.

But she was only partway through putting it on when she heard a loud, crashing thunk and an ensuing, "Oh-oh…"

"Mandy? Are you all right?" Kira shouted, her tension turning to panic just that quick.

Of course the baby didn't answer.

With Mel's diaper half on, half off, Kira snatched her up and ran out of the nursery in search of Mel.

She found the other baby in the bathroom, gleefully splashing the water out of the toilet, clearly remorseless about having knocked the tissue box from the back of the toilet tank into the bathtub, taking with it a bottle of shampoo that was now running down the drain.

"No, Mandy, that's icky," Kira groaned.

She stood Mel on her own two feet to haphazardly

fasten her diaper and then snatched Mandy away from the toilet to wash her hands in the sink.

"You noddy," Mandy decreed during the process.

"Right. I'm the naughty one. The naughty one isn't the stinker who ran away to play in the toilet."

"You sinker," Mandy countered. "Wan Beh-ee."

"Betty isn't here, either," Kira said, feeling disheartened at the reminder that she was not on the list of people the twins wanted taking care of them.

Still, she dried Mandy's hands and arms, trying to believe that the babies would come to like her eventually.

"Okay, now let's change your diaper," she said when she'd finished, as if they were embarking on a great adventure.

But that particular adventure couldn't begin immediately because then she realized that Mel wasn't where she'd set her only moments before. Mel was no longer in the bathroom at all.

"Oh, no," Kira said, thinking that they were like scurrying little mice—the minute their feet hit the floor they took off.

Why hadn't this happened the day before when Cutty had taken care of them? she asked herself.

Then she recalled that whenever he'd had to concentrate on them one at a time, he'd put the other one in the playpen downstairs. Or in a high chair, or in one of the cribs. Or he'd closed the nursery door.

"Containment—that's the first lesson of the day," she said.

Ignoring Mandy's demand to be put down and her

attempt to wiggle out of Kira's arms, Kira took her to search for Mel.

"Da? Da?"

Kira followed the sound of the tiny voice to Cutty's bedroom. Mel was apparently looking there for her father.

"He's not here, honey," Kira informed the little girl from the doorway.

Kira didn't want to go into Cutty's room with it's mahogany furniture and the king-size bed he'd already made up for the day and covered with a plain blue spread. It was his *bedroom* after all. Where he changed his clothes. Where he slept. Where he put on that clean-smelling aftershave that reminded Kira of the ocean and still lingered in the air. It just seemed too intimate a place for her to trespass.

But of course Mel wouldn't come out when Kira asked her to and Kira was left with no choice but to go all the way into the room and catch the baby who made a dash for Cutty's bathroom when she saw Kira coming.

With Mandy in her arms and Mel by the hand, Kira hurried out of the bedroom and back to the nursery for Mandy's diaper change.

This time Kira closed the nursery door, locking herself in with both girls protesting just the way they had the day before anytime she'd tried to take care of them.

"So much for bonding with me when there's no one else around," she muttered to herself.

Fully aware that this was only the beginning of the day.

And that she hadn't miraculously gotten any better at baby wrangling overnight.

"Oh, no, Mandy, how did you get up there?"

Kira's whisper was a lament as she turned in response to the thud she heard behind her.

After an entire day of more mishaps with the twins, the fact that Mandy had climbed from one of the kitchen chairs onto the table and knocked over a gallon of milk was one more rung on the ladder of frustration that evening.

Kira made a dive for the milk carton and for the baby, but by the time she'd righted the container, a good portion of it had flooded out onto the table, run over the side and was dripping onto the floor.

But Kira could hardly get mad at the baby since it was her own fault. She'd been putting Mel in one of the high chairs—a task which ordinarily would only have taken a minute. Only rather than doing it quickly, before Mandy could get into mischief, Kira's attention had wandered—along with her eyes—through the archway that connected the kitchen to the living room.

The living room where Cutty was with the Northbridge College newspaper reporter who had come to interview him. And Kira was having trouble keeping herself from being nosy about it even though she was supposed to be giving the twins crackers and milk to occupy them.

Now she had no choice but to focus on the girls. And the latest mess that had left the kitchen looking every bit as bad as it had before she'd cleaned it spotlessly at dawn this morning.

With Mandy in tow, Kira grabbed a dish towel and tried to staunch the flow of milk onto the floor, leaving it like a dam on the table while she put Mandy into the second high chair.

As she did she couldn't keep her gaze from drifting once more out to the living room where Cutty sat on the couch and the very attractive graduate student was half interviewing him, half flirting with him.

Of course Kira knew it shouldn't make the slightest bit of difference to her. So what if some woman was flirting with him? So what if the woman was tall and thin enough to be a model, or had full, wavy platinum-blond hair that fell to the middle of her back, and breasts at least two cup sizes bigger than hers? It meant nothing to Kira. She was only here for the twins. What Cutty did was Cutty's business. She just hoped he could see through that phony little giggle. And that overly rapt interest.

Who did that woman think she was fooling with those coy glances from under her lashes? And that slow smile with all those ultrabright white teeth?

"I'll bet she practiced that in the mirror for weeks before she had it just right," Kira muttered.

Was Cutty buying it?

He was smiling back. Laughing at something she'd said. That laugh Kira liked so much.

He'd spruced himself up in anticipation of this—

that didn't sit well with her, either. He'd gone upstairs after dinner and put on a clean, pale blue sport shirt with his jeans. He'd shaved, too. And come back down smelling of aftershave.

Kira wished she'd been able to do that. Well, not shave and splash on aftershave. But she wished she'd been able to change out of the wrinkled linen slacks and equally creased camp shirt she'd had on since five-thirty this morning.

Yes, she'd managed to keep from having food spilled on her today, but that was the best she could say about her appearance. Even if she'd made sure her hair would stay in the ponytail at her crown by putting a rubber band on it rather than merely tying it up with a scarf, it would still have been nice to have had the chance to smooth it a little.

Plus, what harm could there have been in refreshing her blush? Or applying some lipstick for the evening? But no, there she was, bare lipped, probably pale, dressed in wilting clothes, while the other woman looked as if she'd just come from a spa.

And wasn't she using it all to good effect? Flipping that remarkable platinum hair around. Bending over to brace her elbows on her knees as if she was so fascinated with Cutty's every word. Showing eye-popping cleavage from the scoop neck of her tank top.

"We don't like her," Kira whispered to the girls as she finally broke a graham cracker in half and gave one to each of them.

"Mik," Mandy reminded then, and only then did Kira recall the spilled milk.

It had soaked through the dish towel and continued to run down the table leg onto the floor. It had also spread to the center of the table and dripped through the crack where the table separated to accommodate a leaf, adding a second puddle underneath, too.

Kira sighed. "She's out there being Miss Wonderful, and I'm in here just messing up again."

"Who's being Miss Wonderful?"

Kira nearly jumped out of her skin.

She spun around and discovered the source of her fright—there was a man standing on the other side of the back screen door.

"You scared me to death," she said.

Apparently feeling at home here, the man opened the screen and came in without an invitation. "Sorry."

He was a tall, good-looking son of a gun with a blinding smile that said he wasn't all *that* sorry.

He held out his hand to her to shake and said, "Ad Walker. I promised Cutty I'd stop by tonight to help you keep the twins corralled."

Kira accepted his hand and replied, "Kira Wentworth."

"Marla's sister. I know."

She knew who Ad Walker was, too. He was the man who had rushed into the burning house with Cutty. The man who Cutty had dragged from the inferno after Ad had been knocked unconscious.

"It's nice to meet you," Kira said. Then, to let him know she was aware of who he was, she added, "I read about you and Cutty in a Denver newspaper. I'm glad to see you don't have any lingering effects of the fire.''

''No, no broken bones. Just a bump on the head,'' he said as if he'd taken it in stride when Kira knew he'd spent two days in the hospital.

He pointed his chin in the direction of the living room then. ''I did my part of this interview a few days ago so I recognized Sherry when I saw her through the front window. I came around back so I wouldn't interrupt them.''

''Ah.''

There was something about the way he was looking at her that convinced Kira he was comparing her to Marla. And just that quick she was once again the geeky, awkward younger sister with braces on her teeth.

Trying to escape feeling inferior, she turned away to pour the babies two sippy-cups of milk.

That seemed to draw Ad Walker's attention away from her, to the milk mess, and then to the rest of the kitchen.

''Holy smoke. I thought Cutty said you were in here early this morning cleaning this place?''

''I was. And I had it in good shape, too. Believe it or not.'' It was just that then the twins had been turned loose for the day and breakfast, lunch and dinner dishes had ended up stacked in the sink and on the counters because Kira had been so overwhelmed once again by her young charges. And now the milk had spilled, so it didn't seem as if she'd done anything.

But Kira was less interested in explaining all that than in the fact that Cutty had talked to his friend about her.

"So why would Cutty tell you I was here early this morning?" she said as she wiped off the milk container and put it back in the fridge.

"He just mentioned it in passing."

Kira had been hoping to learn what exactly Cutty had said about her—if he'd said she didn't compare to Marla in the housekeeping department—and why he'd been talking about her at all.

But Ad Walker didn't seem inclined to say any more. Instead he turned to Mel and Mandy and greeted them with an affectionate and enthusiastic, "How're my girls?"

Both babies tilted their heads back so he could bend over and give them each a kiss on the cheek.

It was cute and funny and it made Kira laugh. "Have you trained them or have they trained you?"

"What can I say? They're just two little flirts," he responded.

As he pretended to taste the soggy cracker Mel offered him a bite of, Kira began working on the spilled milk.

Whether to escape or merely to help out, he excused himself from the twins, left them to their snack and pitched in.

"How long has Sherry been here?" he asked in the process.

"Only about fifteen minutes," Kira answered.

"And already you think she's Miss Wonderful?"

Back to that.

But Kira could tell he was teasing her and she wasn't about to let him get the best of her.

"Well, from a man's point of view, isn't she?" she countered with a nod toward the living room.

Ad craned his neck for another look. "I don't know if wonderful is the word."

"What word would you use? Hot? Gorgeous? Built like a brick house? Or just stacked?"

Why had she said that?

It was his turn to laugh. "You sound a little jealous."

"Me? That's crazy."

"Uh-huh," he said as if he knew better. "You can relax. She isn't his type."

"Whose type?" Kira asked, pretending she didn't know he was referring to Cutty.

"Our boy out there."

"It wouldn't make any difference to me if she was," she said, careful to make it sound as if she meant it.

But Ad Walker didn't seem convinced. He just said another knowing, "Uh-huh."

"Really. I'm not jealous. I just hate to see Cutty sucked in by someone who obviously has more on her agenda than an article for a college newspaper."

For the third time Ad Walker repeated, "Uh-huh."

Kira decided it was easier to change the subject than to fight this.

"I think we better move the table so I can clean

under the leg. If I only clean around it, it's going to stick to the floor.''

Ad obliged her, tipping the table so she could also wash the leg itself and under the center where the milk had dripped through.

Then he moved the table completely out of the way so she had free access to both puddles on the floor.

When she was finished she helped him slide the table back where she thought it had been originally.

''Marla said it had to be exactly under the overhead light,'' Ad explained, adjusting it from two angles before he was satisfied.

Kira thought it would leave more room if it was centered in the room rather than under the light but she didn't say anything. Marla's house. Marla's things. Marla's way.

''More cacker,'' Mandy demanded then.

Kira gave her one half of a second cracker and gave Mel the other half.

''How long does this interview take?'' she asked her assistant.

He shrugged a shoulder and went to the sink to rinse some of the dishes piled high there. ''I was with Sherry for about an hour and a half but I guess it depends on how deep into Cutty's background she wants to go. He might have more to tell. He's an interesting guy, you know.''

Kira opened the dishwasher and began to load the rinsed dishes. ''Actually, I don't know anything about him. Marla didn't bring him around or even confide in me. The first time I knew he existed was the night they both came to the house to tell our parents she was pregnant. Then they eloped and from that point on my father referred to him as the…person…who had ruined Marla.''

"Person?'' Ad repeated. "I'm guessing you deleted the expletive?''

"Many,'' Kira admitted. "The nicest thing he ever called Cutty was trash.''

"Cutty is anything but trash,'' Ad defended as if he couldn't believe anyone had ever thought such a thing about his friend.

"I know. But to my father—''

"Things happen, that's what makes us all human,'' Ad interrupted, still in Cutty's defense. "I didn't know him before he was seventeen but since then the Cutty I've known is a guy who's worked hard—under circumstances that might have broken anyone else—to make the best of himself and tough situations.''

"I don't doubt it,'' Kira assured him, meaning it. From what little she'd seen of Cutty in the short time she'd been in Northbridge she already knew he wasn't the depraved degenerate her father had always made him out to be.

But still Ad seemed to feel the need to convince her. "For my money, you won't find a better man anywhere. People around here give most of the credit to Marla for everything but the truth is, if it hadn't been for Cutty—''

Ad cut himself off this time, as if he might be on

the verge of saying something he'd had second thoughts about.

Then, instead, he said, "I don't want to tell tales out of school. Let's just say that Marla and Cutty had a rough go of it, but Cutty had a rough go of it even before he met Marla."

"He did?" Kira said with uncamouflaged surprise as it struck her for the first time that not only didn't she know anything but the basics about Marla and Cutty after they'd eloped, she also knew absolutely nothing about Cutty before that. About his family or where they'd stood on the whole teenage pregnancy issue or if they were still in his life.

And she suddenly realized she wanted to.

But it didn't look as if she was going to be filled in by Ad because just then Mel shouted, "Wan down," and held out her arms to the big man.

"I think I'm being paged," he said in response. "How about if I take them into the yard to play for a few minutes and then we'll get them to bed?"

"Wanna pay," Mandy chimed in to make sure he knew she wouldn't stand for being left out.

"Sure," Kira agreed.

She helped him take the twins from their high chairs and watched as he herded them outside, pleased to see that despite the fact that they obviously liked Ad, they didn't want any more of his assistance than they did of hers, that they were just independent little things.

But once Kira was alone in the kitchen she again began to wonder about Cutty.

Particularly about why he'd had a *rough go of it* even before he'd met Marla.

And out of that was born a determination to have her curiosity satisfied.

Ad helped Kira get the twins to bed but that was too big a task to allow for any opportunity to question him about what he knew of Cutty. And once the girls were snugly tucked in for the night, he said he had to get back to his restaurant and he left the way he'd come in—through the kitchen door.

Kira could have slipped out, too, and gone to the garage apartment for what remained of the evening. But that was about the last thing she wanted to do because it meant that the few words she'd exchanged with Cutty during the day, the little time she'd had with him, would be all she ended up with.

Not to mention it would also mean that she would have no chance of learning more about Cutty and that she would be leaving him alone with Miss Wonderful.

So she didn't follow Ad out the back door and go to the garage apartment.

Instead she folded the day's laundry and finished cleaning the kitchen, all the while willing the reporter to leave.

She didn't get her wish until nearly ten o'clock but by then the kitchen was sparkling.

"Wow," Cutty said when he limped in after letting the reporter out the front door. "You worked overtime in here."

Kira could hardly say she'd done it to avoid ending

the day without getting to talk to him, so she didn't acknowledge the comment at all.

In lieu of that she said, "You must be dry after so much talking. Can I get you a glass of iced tea?"

"Only if you'll sit and have one with me."

It pleased her more than she wanted to think about that he'd come from being with the other woman and still seemed to want to be with her.

"Sounds good," she said, taking two glasses from the cupboard and pouring tea from a pitcher in the refrigerator.

"The girls got to bed without too much problem?" Cutty asked then.

"With the help of your friend."

"Ad—yeah, I saw him come and go through here."

"He didn't want to interrupt your interview," Kira said.

"I wish he would have. I think that woman was hitting on me."

"And you wanted to share the joy?"

"No, I could have used the protection," Cutty said with a laugh. "Getting married at seventeen doesn't leave you experienced at this stuff. Besides, I think she was a barracuda."

Okay, so maybe what Kira had been experiencing *was* jealousy, because hearing that Cutty hadn't been taken in by the other woman went a long way in improving her mood. And giving her a surprising sense of relief that she was a little afraid to explore.

She brought the two glasses of tea to the table, pulled out a second chair for Cutty to prop his foot on, and then sat across from him on a third ladder-back chair.

"Mel and Mandy seemed more cooperative today," he observed then.

"I'm still not their favorite person but they seem to be tolerating me."

"Thanks for all the work you did on the living room during their nap this afternoon. The Barracuda never guessed that there hadn't even been a place to sit earlier."

"I'm just glad I actually got some things accomplished today," Kira said, letting her relief over that sound in her voice.

Cutty didn't comment. He merely took a drink of his tea.

Kira did, too, wondering all the while how she was going to get into the subject she really wanted to be talking about.

As she searched for a segue she couldn't help surreptitiously studying him.

The one thing she decided she couldn't fault the reporter for was being attracted to him. He was such an appealing combination—rugged, sexy masculinity and the kind of sensitivity that made him seem accessible and genuinely caring.

Then, too, there was the fact that he was jaw-droppingly handsome with a face of chiseled planes and those long-lashed evergreen eyes....

"So, you and Ad seemed to have a lot to talk about in here tonight," he said then, drawing her out of her reverie.

Was she mistaken or was there an edge of something that almost sounded like jealousy in *his* voice?

She couldn't be sure but just the possibility gave her a whole new lease on life.

"Mainly we were talking about you," she said, seizing the opening his comment gave her rather than playing coy.

"If you were talking about me it must have been a boring conversation."

"As a matter of fact, Ad said he didn't know how long the interview would take because you're an interesting person."

"I think he was putting you on."

"I don't think so. But it did occur to me when he said it that I don't really know much about you."

Cutty shrugged, conceding that point. "There's not much reason you *would* know anything about me."

"I'd like to, though," Kira said, jumping in with both feet.

Cutty's mouth slid into a crooked smile that looked pleased to hear it. "You would?"

"I would. Ad said that you had a rough go of it— his words—even before you met Marla. Is that true?" Kira asked.

"I didn't have a storybook childhood, if that's what he was referring to," Cutty admitted, but without a hint of self-pity.

"What kind of childhood *did* you have?"

"In a nutshell, my mother walked out when I was a baby, so I never knew her. And my father was an alcoholic. Not a functional, social-drinker kind of alcoholic. We're talking the town-drunk kind of alcoholic.''

"Really? Was he like that before your mother left or did his drinking come after that?"

"I don't know to tell you the truth. I only know that from my earliest memories he spent more time drunk than sober."

"Did he hold down a job?"

"Off and on. He'd dry out—to him that meant he only drank at night and on the weekends. When he was doing that he'd get whatever job he could. But it would only last a few weeks, a month maybe, before the Friday night binge didn't end on Sunday. Then he'd lose the job. Disappear for days on end—''

"Disappear?"

"He wouldn't come home and I wouldn't know where he was," Cutty explained.

"But he'd leave you with someone, right?"

The question made Cutty laugh a humorless laugh. "Until I was six we rented an attic room in an old house in Denver from a woman named Mabel Brown. Mabel was pretty old but she looked after me, made sure I always had something to eat, a lunch to take to school. But if you're asking if there were formal baby-sitting arrangements made, no, there weren't. Mabel just sort of stepped in when my dad didn't come home."

"But only until you were six?"

"That's when Mabel died. She hadn't owned the house, she'd been renting, too, and using what my father paid her—*when* he paid her—to make her own rent. The owner wasn't happy to discover that and kicked us out. That was when an old army buddy of my dad's let us move into the two rooms above his gas station. Jack was the army buddy and he sort of took over where Mabel had left off. Home-baked cookies were replaced by Vienna sausages,'' Cutty finished with a laugh.

Suddenly Kira's own home life and her harsh father didn't seem so bad.

''Why didn't anyone call Social Services and have you put into a nice home?'' she asked.

''Jack would never have turned my father in for anything. Besides, he lived right behind the station. He just told me whenever my father didn't show up, to knock on his door and I could stay with him. So that's what I did.''

''What about school? Didn't a teacher ever realize what you were going home to?''

''I didn't tell anybody. I was afraid of getting my dad into trouble. Besides, in a lot of ways, it was just how I lived. What I was used to. I didn't really know any different. And if I needed a parent to show up for something at school and my dad wasn't in one of his dry phases, Jack came and told them he was my uncle.''

''What about that—an uncle, I mean. Didn't you say something about an Uncle Paulie?''

''Right. Uncle Paulie. Actually he was my *great*-uncle. But he lived here, in Northbridge and his health wasn't terrific so he never came to visit. He just sent Christmas and birthday cards, and money when my father asked him for loans. He always let me know I was welcome if I ever wanted to move in with him, but he never turned my dad in or anything. You have to understand, as bad as this sounds, my pop was the nicest guy in the world. He was a happy guy, drunk or sober, he was warm and kind and good-hearted. Everybody—including me—loved him. He just had a problem.''

''And you never considered going to stay with your uncle?''

''I had to stick around to take care of my dad,'' Cutty said as if it should have been evident.

''No, your dad should have been taking care of you,'' Kira corrected. ''What about food and clothes? Did he provide those?''

''He'd come home with a sack of groceries whenever he thought of it but they didn't last until the next time it occurred to him so when I'd run out I'd eat with Jack. Plus Jack let me work in the station. I'd sweep up. Stack cans of oil. Keep the counter stocked with gum and candy bars—whatever I could do as a little kid. He'd pay me and I'd stash the cash and use it for stuff to eat here and there.''

''And clothes?''

''Once a year, the day before school started, Jack would take me to the Army Surplus store. He'd buy me two shirts, two pairs of jeans, a package of socks, a package of undershorts, a pair of work boots and a coat if I needed a new one. It was like my employee bonus,'' Cutty said with another laugh.

This story was breaking Kira's heart but Cutty told it as if it was no big deal.

"As I got older," he continued, "Jack taught me how to work on cars and I got to be a pretty good mechanic. So by the time I was a teenager I was making fair money for that. Then I bought my own clothes."

"What happened to your father?" Kira asked then, assuming he was no longer living since Cutty had referred to him in the past tense.

"He died the day before I turned seventeen," Cutty said sadly despite the fact that the man had obviously not been much of a parent to him. "He was drunk, of course, in an alley in downtown Denver. He either passed out or just went to sleep, and froze to death during the night."

Kira didn't know whether to say she was sorry or not. It had been so long ago, that didn't seem called for, so instead she said, "When you were seventeen—did you know Marla then?"

"We were in school together, so I knew her, sure. But we didn't start dating until about a month later. We were put into the same group to do a project in a physics class."

"Were you still living over the gas station?"

"Living and working there," Cutty confirmed.

"So at seventeen you essentially had your own apartment to take a date to," Kira said as one piece fell into place.

"The recipe for disaster," he said, guessing what she was thinking.

But she wasn't only thinking that things might have been different if he and Marla hadn't had quite so much privacy. She was also thinking that she was getting a fuller picture of the young Cutty. A picture that explained some things.

"So from when you were just a little kid you not only had to take care of yourself, but of your father, too," she summarized then. "And even when you had the chance to leave you didn't because you felt like you had to take care of your dad. That sense of responsibility must have played a big part when Marla got pregnant."

Again Cutty shrugged as if that was just a given. "Her being pregnant was my doing," he said.

"And when Marla didn't want to have an abortion, you eloped. Then did you guys both live over the gas station?" Kira asked because she honestly didn't know what had happened to them after that.

"We only stayed at the gas station for a few days. It wasn't a good place for Marla. That was when I finally took Uncle Paulie up on his offer and we came to Northbridge."

He said that with a note of finality in his tone that Kira took to mean he didn't want to talk about what happened then. So even though her curiosity was only partially satisfied, she didn't push it.

Instead it was her turn to say, "Wow."

"Like I said, not a storybook beginning all the way around."

"That's an understatement." And no wonder his friend had been so defensive on his behalf. It was amazing that after growing up the way he had, Cutty was the man he was.

And what a man he was sitting across from her, calm, strong, confident. And so attractive. Even more attractive—if that were possible—now that she knew all he'd gone through, all he'd overcome and risen above.

"I should probably go," she said suddenly when she realized that their eyes had been locked together for a few minutes for no reason she could explain.

Cutty didn't say anything. He merely went on watching her.

Kira stood and took both of their empty glasses to the sink to rinse and put in the dishwasher.

When she turned again he was standing, bracing part of his weight on his cane, tall and straight, with those broad shoulders and that slightly disheveled hair and those eyes still on her.

"Tomorrow I'd like to use nap time to get myself some more practical clothes," she said then, in a hurry to inject something mundane into what suddenly seemed charged and somehow sensual. "Jeans. T-shirts. I didn't pack with the twins in mind."

Cutty was slow to pick up the ball but after another moment of feeling as if his gaze was caressing her, he seemed to concede and said, "There are a couple of small stores on the main drag and one department store near the college. I'll give you directions."

"Okay. Thanks."

Kira knew she needed to leave but it wasn't easy to force her feet to take her to the door.

"I guess I'll see you in the morning then," she said, hoping to give herself more impetus.

"And you can sleep in a little since the kitchen and living room are clean," Cutty pointed out as he followed her to the screen.

"Right," she agreed. "Except the place could use some dusting and vacuuming and mopping. And I didn't get to the laundry today and—"

They were suddenly standing face-to-face at the door and Cutty had raised a single index finger to her lips to stop the flow of her lengthening to-do list.

He was studying her intently, his green eyes holding her so mesmerized that even when he took his finger away, she still didn't go on.

"I'm just grateful for what you did today," he said in a voice that was deeper, softer, richer than the simple statement seemed to warrant.

Kira forced herself out of the near trance he'd put her into and tried to joke. "I'm just glad I actually *did* something."

He didn't laugh. But then neither did she. Instead they both seemed lost in something Kira didn't quite understand. Something that the touch of that finger to her lips, that look in his eyes, had caused. But whatever it was, from what it was making her feel, she knew she should cut it short before it completely carried her away.

Cutty surprised her then by bending down enough to replace that index finger with his lips, kissing her.

It was quick. There and gone before she so much as closed her eyes. Or kissed him back.

But it was a kiss nonetheless.

"For a job well-done," he said then, making a joke of his own to explain what seemed to have taken him a little by surprise, too.

"Better than a package of socks from Army Surplus," she countered.

It made him laugh, and Kira liked that. And him. More than she thought she should.

So, rather than potentially making a fool of herself, she pushed open the screen door and stepped outside, refusing to look up at that face that had too powerful an effect on her.

"I'll see you tomorrow," she said as she did.

"I'll be here."

He'd clearly only meant that offhandedly but it was enough to make it easier for Kira to leave him and cross the yard to the garage apartment.

Because without the thought that she would get to see him again in only a matter of hours, she might not have been able to make herself go.

Chapter Four

The kiss Cutty had given Kira was the last thing she thought about when she went to bed Friday night and the first thing on her mind when she woke up Saturday morning. She couldn't stop thinking about it. No matter how hard she tried. And she *did* try.

But for some reason, there wasn't a single thing that was capable of distracting her from it. From thinking about that little nothing-of-a-kiss.

Why had he kissed her? she asked herself for the dozenth time as she got out of bed and headed for the shower.

He'd said that it was only a reward for a job well-done and it had sounded like a joke, but maybe it hadn't been. Maybe the kiss really had only been a friendly sort of gesture, she thought as she stepped under the spray of warm water and let it beat down on her. Maybe that nothing-of-a-kiss had genuinely been nothing. Just a thanks for playing temporary nanny and housekeeper. A nothing-of-a-kiss that could as easily have been on the cheek as on the lips.

Except that it *hadn't* been on the cheek.

It had been on the lips.

And Kira didn't honestly believe that it had only been a thank-you kiss. Not when she factored in the way Cutty had been looking at her just before he'd kissed her. Not when she remembered the feeling she'd had of being lost in those eyes.

No, that kiss—no matter how brief—had been more than a thank-you kiss.

Just not *much* more.

Maybe it had been a test-kiss, she thought, still trying to decipher it and what it might have meant.

A test-kiss. Like dipping an elbow in the babies' bathwater before putting them in the tub.

But if that was the case, then what was Cutty testing? Kira wondered.

Her, maybe. Maybe he was seeing what she would do. If she would slap him. Or be horrified. Or kiss him back.

She hadn't slapped him or been horrified. But she hadn't kissed him back, either. She'd just been too surprised to do anything but stand there.

And she shouldn't be regretting that, she told herself as she shampooed her hair. She shouldn't be regretting that she hadn't done anything to encourage him.

She wished she'd kissed him back. She wished that the kiss had lasted longer than it had.

And it was easy to see why. Cutty was beefcake beautiful. He was nice. Kind. Patient. Intelligent. Funny. He was the real deal. The complete package.

Still, that didn't change the fact that she couldn't give in to his appeal, she reminded herself when her shower was finished. It didn't change the fact that she would never allow herself to be merely some replacement—the way her mother had been for Marla's mother.

It was just that it would have helped if there wasn't something there when it came to Cutty, she thought. Something that made her notice every detail about him. Every nuance. That made her extremely aware of every hair on his head. Of every inch of his face. Of every bulge of every muscle.

It would have helped if there wasn't something there that made her know when he came into a room even if she didn't hear or see him. Something that didn't make her heart flutter each time she caught sight of him. Something that had left her whole body aquiver after that nothing-of-a-kiss…

That nothing-of-a-kiss that he should never have begun, she thought as she discarded the towel she'd used to dry off and slipped into her robe.

Not that she wasn't guilty of thinking about what it might be like to have him kiss her. She was. Yes, there had been the odd moment when he was talking on the telephone and his lips were near the mouthpiece and a momentary image flashed through her mind of those same lips pressed to hers.

Yes, there had been more than one occasion when he'd smiled or laughed and her gaze got caught on those agile lips, lingering there while she wondered what that mouth might feel like on hers, what those lips might feel like parting over hers, urging hers to part, too....

But she was only guilty of thinking about it. Simple, fleeting fantasies that she'd pushed aside almost the moment they happened. Flights of fancy. Certainly not anything she would have ever acted on. At least she didn't believe she would ever have acted on them.

But he had.

And she couldn't deny that even just recalling it was enough to send a little rush through her.

"Stop it," she commanded her reflection in the mirror over the sink while she ran a brush through her hair.

But the rush went on undisturbed anyway.

And that worried Kira. It worried her that Cutty had opened a door that should never have been opened. It worried her that she wasn't going to be able to suppress those fantasies if she thought there was any possibility that they might become more than that.

No, no, no. She didn't even know why she'd thought such a thing.

But that was the trouble—now that he'd kissed her, anything was possible.

Except that she wasn't going to *let* anything be possible, she decided. She wasn't going to let anything else happen.

But what did that mean exactly? Was she going to confront him? Tell him flat-out that he'd better never do that again?

That didn't seem like a good idea. She couldn't think of too many things that would make her more uncomfortable than that. And it would make everything that came after it uncomfortable, too. So uncomfortable that Cutty might not even want her help with the twins anymore. And that would defeat her main purpose for being here.

If he ever tried to kiss her again, she would put a stop to it before it actually happened, that's all.

"And I mean it," she said forcefully to herself.

Because when she got involved with a man it would be with a man who wasn't carrying around someone else's shoes for her to fill, and that's all there was to it.

She took a deep, cleansing breath and blew it out, convinced that she'd reached the right conclusion....

Saturday was as chaotic as every other day so far.

That was good in that it kept Kira too busy to dwell much more on the kiss or have any time alone with Cutty to feel awkward.

But it wasn't so good in that when Kira got the twins down for their naps that afternoon the house was so torn apart that she knew she should use the peace and quiet to clean rather than leaving to go shopping.

Cutty insisted, though, that she have that hour to herself, and since she really needed more practical clothes, she forced herself to turn a blind eye to the toys strewn everywhere; to the mud the twins had tracked into the kitchen; to the juice box Mel had dropped, Mandy had stepped on, and Kira had only superficially mopped up; and to the laundry that had yet to be done.

"Okay, but I'll be back before the girls wake up and I'll stay as long as I need to tonight," Kira assured Cutty, concerned that she would still just be doing surface cleaning when she was dying to scrub the place from top to bottom the way she had no doubt Marla would have done by now.

"Take your time," Cutty responded, handing over directions he'd written out for her to the department store near the college.

Kira was actually hoping she wouldn't need to go that far, that between the two boutiques on Main Street she would be able to get what she needed. But she accepted the slip of paper anyway, careful not to touch his hand when she did to avoid the effect any kind of contact had on her.

The first shop stocked mainly gauzy, free-flowing dresses, skirts and vests that weren't any more suitable for chasing the twins than the linens and silks Kira had packed. So that was a complete bust.

But the second shop had a wider selection of just what she was looking for.

She was only at the beginning of her browse when a saleswoman who looked to be Betty the housekeeper's age approached her.

"Am I mistaken or are you Marla Grant's sister?" the woman asked.

Kira stopped sorting through jeans to glance at the tall, slender woman with the gunmetal-gray hair cut short and compensated for with large onyx earrings dangling from her lobes. "Yes, I'm Marla's sister."

"I thought so. I know Betty Cunningham and she told me all about you coming in to help Cutty with the twins. I think that's so nice."

This really was a small town.

"I didn't actually come in to help out," Kira amended.

"But you stayed when you saw the need and that's what counts."

"It's really nothing," Kira demurred.

"We all think you're just a godsend," the woman insisted.

Kira didn't know who *we all* was but she felt guilty for being considered a godsend when she was so bad at the job she'd undertaken. She also hated to think of the talk that would follow when Betty came back to work, discovered how inept she'd been and told *we all*.

"Are you looking for a gift?" the woman asked then, when Kira glanced back at the jeans.

"No, I'm just looking for a few things to supplement what I brought with me."

"Well, these are the plus sizes and you're no bigger than a minute. You need the other side of the aisle. Let me show you.''

As Kira followed her, the woman said, ''My name is Carol, by the way. And Betty said you're Kira.''

''Nice to meet you.''

''You know, we just loved your sister,'' Carol informed her as Kira chose two pairs of jeans in her size and moved to a rack of knit tops. ''We all thought she was a saint, pure and simple. The nicest girl in the world and so beautiful on top of it all. Never a hair out of place on that one.''

Kira suddenly wondered if her own hair had slipped out of the rubber band that held it low on her nape today.

But what she said was, ''I loved her, too.''

''We all were just heartsick about her,'' Carol added. ''That accident was a horrible, horrible thing.''

''Yes,'' was all Kira could say. This was not an easy thing for her to talk about, especially with someone she didn't know.

''But we all think Cutty is doing better now and it helps that he has those babies. They just couldn't be cuter,'' the older woman said on a lighter note.

''They are adorable,'' Kira agreed, moving along the rack of T-shirts.

But as she did Marla was less on her mind than was the reporter from the night before. And she found herself drawn to a black tank top that was closer to what the reporter had had on than to anything.

No, that wasn't a good choice, she lectured herself. Especially now, when she was doing so much lifting and carrying and bending over. Definitely not a good choice. She didn't even know why she was considering it. It wasn't as if she ordinarily wore things like that.

So back went the tank top to the rack and she picked up a V-neck with cap sleeves instead.

"I think I would have known you were Marla's sister even if Betty hadn't described you," Carol was saying. "You're every bit as pretty as she was. You girls must have come from good genes."

Kira didn't want to embarrass the woman by telling her she and Marla hadn't been related by blood so she merely thanked her for the compliment.

Then, deciding that the jeans and the four T-shirts she'd picked out were enough, Kira let the saleswoman know she had what she needed.

But as Carol led the way to the cash register, Kira started to think about that tank top again.

She knew she really shouldn't buy it. It would be tight fitting. And low cut.

But it would also be cool...

"Let me get you totaled up," Carol said.

Now or never...

"Oh, just a minute," Kira heard herself say before she realized she was going to.

Then, as if her feet had a will of their own, she made a quick dash to the rack and grabbed that black tank top anyway, bringing it back with her to the counter.

And all the while Carol was ringing her up and continuing to talk about how unbelievable Marla had been, Kira just stood there wondering if the sales-woman was thinking that the tank top was not only not something Marla would have bought, but that it was also something Kira shouldn't be wearing around Cutty.

Or if that was just what Kira was thinking.

The house was quiet when Kira got back. She came in the front door and when she didn't find Cutty in either the living room or the kitchen, she assumed he was upstairs dealing with the end of nap time.

But in case the twins were still sleeping, she didn't call for him. Instead she put the bag that held her new clothes out of Mel's and Mandy's reach on top of the refrigerator and went up the stairs.

When she got to the second floor, though, she didn't find Cutty in the nursery. In fact the nursery door wasn't open at all. But another door was. The door that hadn't been open the entire time Kira had been there. The door Betty had pointed out to her as the door to Anthony's room.

Kira wasn't exactly sure what to do. She was already there and if Cutty had heard her coming it would seem weird now for her to slink back down-stairs without saying anything. But she was also worried that if he was in that room, he might not want to be disturbed.

In the end she decided to make a beeline past the open bedroom door to the laundry closet as if doing the wash was the reason she'd come up in the first place. She thought it would give Cutty the opportunity to close the door for privacy if he didn't want to be interrupted.

The trouble was, she couldn't keep herself from sneaking a peek as she neared that room.

Sure enough, Cutty was inside, holding a very raggedy stuffed dog and staring at it so remorsefully that Kira's heart just ached for him. Too much to ignore him and merely do laundry, even if she was disturbing him.

"Are you all right?" she whispered.

He raised his gaze slowly from the stained and soiled toy and gave Kira a sad sort of smile. "Oh, hi. I didn't know you were back."

"I'm sorry. I didn't mean to bother you. I—"

"It's okay. You aren't bothering me. I wasn't really doing anything. I heard one of the girls waking up and I didn't think I should wait to start the climb up the stairs since I'm so slow at it. By the time I got here things were quiet again but you know that won't last long. I didn't want to go all the way down the stairs again and have to come back up them, so I thought I'd take a look at what needs to be done in here while I waited for them to wake up completely."

Kira nodded, understanding that he needed to keep his trips up and down the stairs to a minimum.

"If you'd rather be alone—" she said then.

Cutty shook his head. "No, that's okay. Come on in."

She accepted the invitation and went into the empty room with him, taking a look around.

If someone had said a war had been waged in the

small space she wouldn't have been surprised. There were holes in the walls, pieces of wallboard had been peeled off and scratches and scuff marks marred the paint everywhere.

"Betty told me this was Anthony's room," she said somewhat tentatively because she wasn't sure she should bring it up.

But Cutty didn't seem to mind. "Yep, this was it. Not a pretty picture, is it?"

Kira didn't answer that but he continued anyway. "Anthony was kind of tough on his surroundings," he said, sounding as sad as his smile had looked. "We kept a football helmet on him for when he would bang his head. Steel-toed boots for when he'd be in kicking mode. There was only a mattress on the floor so he wouldn't get hurt. But there wasn't much we could do for the walls or the paint."

"Did he bang his head and kick often?" Kira asked.

"It wasn't unusual," Cutty said.

Neither of them said anything for a moment.

Then Kira confessed, "I wonder about him. What he was like."

"He was…I don't know. He was Anthony. A little boy locked in his own world. A world he didn't like disturbed."

Kira wasn't sure Cutty wanted to talk about this when he paused for a long while so she didn't say more to prompt him.

But then he went on anyway, as if he'd just been

trying to think of other ways to let her know her nephew.

"Anthony never spoke a word. Ever. But he loved music. In fact, he loved it so much that sometimes when he would get into one of his…rages…I'd sing to him and it would calm him down. Of course the flip side of his loving music was that he would get on these humming jags. One song. Every waking hour. For days on end."

"Oh dear."

"Oh dear is right."

"Was the dog his favorite toy?" Kira asked then, nodding at the ratty stuffed animal.

"That's kind of hard to say. Anthony didn't form attachments to much of anything. But repetition is an element of autism. Like the humming, there were things he just did—for no reason—over and over again. One of those things was that he'd sit in the corner and rub the dog back and forth on the floor—like a scrubbing sponge. For Anthony that was as close as it came to being his favorite toy."

"So, if he didn't form attachments to anything, does that mean he didn't form attachments to you or to Marla, either?"

"That's what it means. He didn't like to be touched. Physical contact was one of the things that would set off the self-harm, so we had to keep it strictly to bathing him, washing his hair—only what absolutely had to be done. The music helped there, too, though," Cutty added.

There was a note in his voice when he said it that

told Kira that no matter how difficult it had been to care for Anthony, Cutty had done it lovingly.

"You miss him, don't you? In spite of the bad things," she said then.

"Sure," Cutty said simply. "In spite of everything he was still my boy."

Cutty's voice cracked almost imperceptibly and he turned his back to Kira to set the toy on the window ledge, making sure it was just so—maybe the way Anthony had wanted it. Or Marla.

For a long moment he stayed there, staring at the stuffed dog, and Kira could only hope he had some good memories to help ease the obvious sorrow of his loss.

When he turned back to her again his expression was more serene. "Sounds like the girls are awake."

The soft baby chatter Mel and Mandy sometimes engaged in was coming from the nursery but it hadn't penetrated Kira's thoughts as she'd witnessed Cutty's grief. Now that he'd brought it to her attention, she dragged herself out of her own reverie.

"I'll get them. Go ahead downstairs and get off your ankle."

"I'm a slave to the ankle," he said wryly. "What do you say we break free of our chains for a little while tonight?"

She didn't know what he was suggesting, and her expression must have given her away because he explained.

"If I didn't have this bad foot I'd be playing softball tonight. How about if we pack up the girls and go watch the game? There'll be plenty of hands to help out with them once we get there, and it'll do us all good."

"I shouldn't," Kira said in a hurry.

It wasn't that she didn't want to go. She did. She *really* did. Which was reason enough not to do it because then she'd be giving in to the desire to spend time with Cutty. Plus there was the fact that if she went she wouldn't get her work around the house done and she would have yet another day of housekeeping failure under her belt.

"I was going to get this place cleaned up, remember?" she said. "And maybe even actually dust and vacuum."

"Work instead of play," he summarized, sounding disappointed.

Kira assumed his disappointment was for himself, that he was figuring if she didn't go, he couldn't, either. So she tried to fix that. "That doesn't mean you can't go. I can keep the girls and just clean after they go to bed."

"You'd actually miss a softball game on a beautiful summer night—a *Saturday* night—to *clean?*" he countered as if that were unthinkable.

"The place really needs it. I'm living in fear of someone dropping by and seeing what a bad job I'm doing."

"Everybody needs some recreation," Cutty persisted with all his charm.

Kira wasn't a sports fan by any stretch of the

imagination, but the thought of an evening out in the summer air, with Cutty, *was* pretty appealing.

Still, she repeated, "I shouldn't," and reinforced it with thoughts of Betty and Carol realizing how inferior she was to Marla.

"The messes aren't going anywhere. They'll all be here when you get back," he reminded.

"Exactly."

"Come on," he cajoled in a sort of singsong.

There wasn't a doubt in Kira's mind that Marla wouldn't have gone off to a softball game and left her house in the shape it was in. It was something their father would never have allowed. Something Kira would never have done herself at home. But oh, it was tempting.

"Will you go even if I don't?" she asked.

He grinned as if he'd seen the loophole. "No, I'd stay cooped up here, going stir-crazy. And it would be all your fault."

Kira knew he was teasing her, and that he could very well go without her just the way he'd been able to go on his own to see Ad the day before. She also recognized that going to a softball game with him was hardly in the line of duty for her. That it was almost like a date. And that dating Cutty was the last thing she should be doing.

"Come on," he repeated, "The house will wait. But this is your only chance today to see a game."

There he was, standing so tall and gorgeous and sexy, and he was just so difficult to say no to...

"Okay," she finally conceded. "But if word gets

around that I'm slacking off on the job it's your fault."

He laughed. "My lips are sealed."

And soft and smooth and warm...

But that was definitely not a thought Kira wanted to have so she pushed it aside.

It was bad enough that she'd just agreed to overlook the job she was supposed to be doing for an outing with him. The last thing she needed was to start thinking about that kiss again, too.

"Who's playing this softball game tonight?" Kira asked Cutty as they worked on opposite sides of the family station wagon to get Mel and Mandy into the car seats in the back seat after dinner that night.

"We're the Northbridge Bruisers," he answered with an exaggerated cheerleading quality to his tone.

"Is it Little League?"

That made him laugh. "No, we're all big boys. There's about twenty of us—all grown-up—who have a sort of league of our own, I guess you could call it. What we do is divide up into two teams by picking names out of a hat—so the teams vary every game to keep it interesting. Then we play softball in the spring and summer, flag football in the autumn and basketball during the winter. It's just for fun and exercise."

"Who are the twenty guys?"

"I'm one. And Ad and his brothers—he has three of them—play. The other fifteen are...well, just Northbridge guys. They run the gamut—we have the younger of our two doctors, our dentist, the local contractor, one guy and his brother who own a ranch outside of town. We're all just—''

"Northbridge guys," Kira finished for him.

"Right."

"And you always only play each other?"

"Most of the time. Every now and then some of the college guys or some of the high-school kids will get together and challenge us to a game. There aren't enough of them at either place to have their own official teams, but they try to give us a run for our money once in a while. For the most part, though, yes, we just compete against each other. Like I said, it's only for fun and exercise.''

Maybe that was what kept him in such good shape, Kira thought, sneaking a peek at him as she clicked Mandy's seat belt into place.

He'd put on a pair of less-faded jeans and a white Henley T-shirt that hugged every muscle of his honed chest, his broad shoulders, his hard biceps. He was clean shaven and smelled heavenly, and Kira knew she was way too happy to be leaving housework behind in favor of spending the evening with him. But she was trying not to dwell on it. Trying to tell herself that there was nothing more to it than a group outing.

"The college must be really small if there aren't sports teams," she said when she realized that silence had fallen while she'd been surreptitiously ogling him.

Cutty didn't seem to have noticed. "Very small. They only have about two hundred students at any given time.''

"That's tiny."

"It's a private college that was founded mainly for people out here in the sticks. First priority for acceptance is given to people who live in the small, rural communities."

With the twins all strapped in, Cutty limped to the driver's side while Kira got into the passenger's seat. Even though she'd ventured out to the two boutiques on Main Street that afternoon, she still hadn't seen much of Northbridge so Cutty had offered to give her the nickel tour before going to the game.

Once they were on their way he began at the end of Main Street where Kira had stopped at the gas station for directions the evening she'd arrived.

As he drove, Cutty pointed out what was what and added a few anecdotes along the way.

Kira listened and took in the sights of the small town.

Most of the buildings on Main Street were built in the early 1900s. Two and three stories tall, they were lined up without any space between them, and with more attention paid to their brick facades than to what was behind those facades.

There was an overhang of some sort from above the first level of almost all the shops, stores and businesses the buildings housed, some with permanent roofing, some with awnings, and some that formed patiolike front pieces that stretched all the way to the street.

The largest building was a four-story redbrick behemoth on the corner of Main Street and Marshall that had originally housed the mercantile. Now it was the medical facility, complete with a five-room hospital.

Northbridge's expansion was obvious as they went farther down Main Street. There the buildings were more boxy than the older models and lacked the character of their predecessors' arches, different-colored-brick outlines and variations in rooflines.

But architecture notwithstanding, the La Brea ice-cream parlor in the glass-fronted shop at the opposite end of Main Street still had a line of customers waiting all the way out the front door.

Main Street ended there in a T. Cutty turned left then, showing Kira the white, tall-steepled church, and, beyond that, the stately blond brick government building that held his office.

The college was farther out, barely on the edges of the city proper. It was a nondescript, flat-walled building that didn't draw much attention from the dormitory that was housed in a stately old mansion that would have done any Ivy League university proud.

Cutty turned the car around in the college parking lot and retraced the T, bypassing Main Street to go east this time. The department store had taken over the corner opposite the ice-cream parlor and past that they drove through small and moderate houses much like the one Cutty owned—all with their own warmth and charm, all at least forty years old, nearly all of them frame with wide porches and homey Victorian touches in their shutters and spindled porch rails.

That took them to the school compound—that's

what Cutty had called it when he'd told her where the softball game was being held.

He'd explained that Northbridge didn't have enough population to sustain separate elementary, junior high and high schools so what had been established instead was a three-building compound that allowed each level a structure of its own to keep the age-groups apart while still sharing a single cafeteria, gymnasium, auditorium, office and combination playground-sports field.

Cutty's own league was allowed use of the gym and the soccer-football-baseball-field-day field for their games.

He parked the car as close as possible to that multipurpose field where the wooden bleachers were already loaded with onlookers.

"You get quite a crowd," Kira observed.

"Friends, family, friends of family—Northbridge is hardly bustling with activities so even small events get a pretty good turnout."

With the engine off and the keys pulled from the ignition, Kira expected that they would be getting out of the car. But instead Cutty angled slightly toward her. And the smile he gave her made it seem as if he knew something she didn't.

"Are you ready for this?" he asked.

Confused, Kira said, "I didn't know there was anything for me to need to be ready for. Do the twins misbehave in public or something?"

"No, they'll be fine. We'll hardly see them. They'll get passed around and spoiled rotten."

"Then what do I need to be ready for?"

"A whole bunch of what you said you ran into today when you went shopping. Everybody's going to want to meet you. And I do mean *everybody*. Northbridge is a lot different than Denver. There aren't any strangers—even with the college in town."

"Today wasn't so bad," Kira said, meaning it even if she had come away feeling inadequate in comparison to Marla again. That just seemed to be her lot in life.

"So you think you can handle it?" Cutty said.

"I think so."

"Okay. Here goes..."

Cutty hadn't been overstating when he'd said that everyone would want to meet her. In the hours that followed getting the twins into their stroller and the slow trek that took them from the parking lot to the field, Kira didn't see much of the softball game. Instead she spent that time meeting and talking to every single person there.

Not that she minded, because she didn't. Everyone was as nice as they could be, and if no one failed to mention Marla and how wonderful, how accomplished, how incredible they thought she was, at least it was good to know that her sister had been so well loved.

It wasn't only Marla who was adored, though, Kira realized as the evening wore on. Or the twins who were fussed over and spoiled. Cutty received more than his share of praise, too.

At first Kira thought it was due to his broken ankle,

but as time went on it became obvious that he was one of Northbridge's fair-haired boys—broken ankle or not. It was almost like being with a celebrity.

When the game was over Cutty declined the invitation to go to Ad's bar and restaurant for the post-game celebration, and he and Kira took the two weary babies home.

It was nearly ten by the time Kira had Mel and Mandy in bed. She headed back downstairs, expecting to find Cutty on the sofa with his ankle elevated on the coffee table. But the living room was empty of all but the toys strewn around it, and the dust and dirt she hadn't yet attended to.

She wondered if he'd gone to bed himself while she'd been busy in the nursery. Although it seemed strange that he might do that without saying good-night.

Still, the mere possibility dashed hopes she hadn't even realized she'd had. Hopes that the evening might not be quite over.

It was that kiss, she thought as she tried to swallow her dejection. Maybe Cutty was avoiding her. Maybe he was worried she would want him to do it again and he didn't want to. Which was silly because of course she didn't want him to do it again. He didn't have to run and hide to avoid it.

Kira had herself worked up into quite a snit by the time she made it to the kitchen.

Then she found Cutty.

He was standing at the sink, slamming back two

aspirin, oblivious to the course her thoughts had just taken.

And Kira's snit evaporated and her hopes reinflated just that quick.

She tried to ignore those hopes, though, and said, "Is your ankle bothering you?"

"A little," he admitted reluctantly.

"Maybe you should get off of it. I'm going to straighten up a few things in here before I call it a night, but if you want to go up to—"

"How about if I just sit here and keep you company?" he said simply enough.

"Okay," she agreed, wishing she hadn't sounded quite so pleased that he was inclined to stay with her.

She watched as Cutty pulled out two of the kitchen chairs—one to sit on and the other to brace his leg, wondering even as she did why it was that she never seemed to tire of looking at him.

Dishes. Do the dishes, she told herself.

She crossed to where he'd been standing moments before and went to work rinsing what was waiting for her in the sink, ignoring the fact that the African-print skirt and silk blouse she'd changed into to go to the game wasn't a great outfit for dishwashing.

"You're pretty popular around here," she said.

Cutty laughed. "Well, since I have to live and work here I hope at least a few people like me."

"There seems to be more to it than just being well liked," Kira said, recalling the affection that had greeted him at the softball game. "It's as if Marla was the favorite daughter, and you're the favorite son.''

"I know Marla was the favorite daughter," he said somewhat under his breath.

"And you are definitely the favorite son," she persisted.

"I suppose that's probably not too far off the mark," he finally conceded. "The whole town did sort of take us under their wing."

"When you first moved here?"

"Soon after. Remember that it's a small town. Everyone knows everyone else's business—sometimes that can be a pain, but other times knowing that business causes folks to pitch in and help."

"There weren't raised eyebrows over two seventeen-year-olds being married and having a baby?"

"Uncle Paulie set the tone. He didn't look at teenagers having a baby as anything but a part of life. In fact he'd always say it only happened to the living, that the dead didn't have to worry about it." Cutty laughed at that. "I'm not sure how that measures up as words of wisdom go, but after your father acting like we'd just single-handedly destroyed the world, that philosophy was a welcome relief."

"And the rest of Northbridge followed his lead?"

"Everybody loved Uncle Paulie. Like my dad, he was one of those guys it's hard not to love. He had a big, boisterous laugh to go with his big, round belly, and he gave away as many doughnuts and coffees as he sold. It didn't hurt that he was in full support of us. Then, too, he told anybody who would listen what kind of a life I'd had growing up, and that Marla's father had turned his back on her—that got a lot of sympathy aimed in our direction. We sort of became the town project in a lot of ways that helped us make it.''

''Money?''

''I worked from the second day we got here—in the doughnut shop—so no, not really so much money. But folks gave us old furniture when we turned the garage into an apartment. And there was a communal baby shower to help us get ready for Anthony. But more important there was just acceptance, helping hands in the way of opportunities offered us, baby-sitting so we could finish high school and so I could go to college at night, things like that. Things that were more neighbor helping neighbor, except that for a long time I couldn't reciprocate.''

''But now you do,'' Kira guessed.

''Every chance I get.''

''Every day in your job,'' she pointed out.

She'd finished the dishes and it was too late to mop the whole floor, so she dampened some paper towels and went to work on the mud trail.

The problem was, she was hardly dressed for cleaning the floor and it wasn't easy to do it and keep her skirt out of the way.

She tried, though, hanging on to the billowy cotton with one hand while she crouched down to wield the paper towel with the other.

''If I was to guess,'' she said as she did, ''I'd say that was why you became a police officer—to give back to the community that gave to you when you needed it.''

''That sounds so cliché,'' he said with a hint of a groan.

''So it isn't true?'' she asked, nearly losing her balance and barely keeping herself from falling flat on her face.

She hoped Cutty hadn't seen it. And maybe he hadn't because he just answered her question.

''It's true that I wanted to do something that helped everybody who helped us. Protect and serve—that seemed to fit the bill. But it's not as if I don't like my job, because I do. I wouldn't want to be doing anything else. And to be honest, I think one of the main factors in my choosing to do it was your father.''

That confused Kira. ''My father?'' she repeated, struggling with her skirt every time she moved forward in the odd sort of duckwalk she was doing.

''I hated that he thought I was some lowlife scum. That I was no good. That I'd never make anything of myself. I think in some ways being a cop was the other extreme and maybe that was part of the appeal.''

''Well, no one around here thinks you're anything but terrific,'' she informed him, thinking that she was glad of that, that he deserved it.

Kira duckwalked forward to the dirty spot right beside Cutty's chair and nearly toppled over once more.

This time Cutty saw it because he said, ''Why

don't you leave that until tomorrow when you aren't in a dress?''

"I'm almost finished," she said as she actually did wipe up the last of the mud.

But then she tried to stand.

And in the process she lost her grip on her skirt, stepped on the hem and the next thing she knew, she'd lurched right into big, strong arms that caught her by reflex.

"Oh!" she cried out in alarm.

After a moment of shock himself, Cutty laughed that deep, rich laugh. "Hello," he said as if she'd intended to end up that way.

Kira tried not to notice the instant wellspring of sparkles that ran all through her at that contact and yanked herself backward, out of his hold.

"I'm sorry," she said, sounding as flustered as she felt.

"Are you okay?" he asked.

"Yes. Are you?"

"As long as you don't count that it's been tough enough keeping my hands off you and you just fell right into my lap."

Had he really just said he was having trouble keeping his hands off her?

That turned up the wattage on those sparkles.

But Kira pretended that wasn't the case and that he hadn't just said what he'd said. "You were right, I shouldn't have been cleaning the floor in a skirt. I should have waited. But no, I just had to do it now.

I just couldn't let it go until tomorrow,'' she said, berating herself.

"No harm done," Cutty assured her.

"But there could have been. What if I'd hit your ankle? What if you'd jerked it yourself?"

"My ankle is fine. Besides," he added with a sly, one-sided grin, "How often does a beautiful woman throw herself at me? Let's just say I fell on you last night, and you fell on me tonight, and call it even."

"Does that mean last night was an accident?" she asked before she'd controlled the tone that made her sound disappointed.

Cutty took his foot off the second chair and stood. Leaving his cane propped against the table, he picked up the paper towel she'd dropped, and on his way to throwing it out he paused to lean close to her ear.

"No, last night was not an accident."

He limped to the trash container, leaving Kira lost for a split second in the warm sensation left in his wake.

Once he'd disposed of the paper towel he turned his backside to the edge of the countertop to rest against it, taking his weight off his broken ankle by propping it atop the unbroken one.

"Although," he said then, "I have to admit I didn't put much thought into that little bit of indiscretion beforehand."

"Did you regret it?" That question had just come out on its own, too.

Cutty laughed. "Not hardly. In fact, I've been thinking all day and night about doing it again."

"You have?"

"I have."

"That's probably not a good idea, though?" she countered in a questioning tone that was much too tentative to carry any weight.

"No, it probably isn't," he agreed just as tentatively. "But good idea or not, every time it pops into my head—every time *you* pop into my head—it seems like something apart from everything and everybody else, and not a damn thing I tell myself makes any difference. I just want to kiss you again anyway."

Those sparkles inside her felt as if they had turned into full beams of light that were setting her aglow.

"It does seem like that—something apart from everything and everybody else," she confessed in a quiet voice.

Cutty's smile turned slow and sexy. "Does that mean if I were to kiss you again you wouldn't hit me over the head with the first thing you could grab?"

He would probably be the first thing she'd want to grab.

But she didn't say that. She said, "We shouldn't." Only somehow it came out sounding like an invitation.

"I know," he agreed, bending at the waist and reaching for her, pulling her to stand in front of him and clasping his hands loosely at the base of her spine so that his forearms rode the sides of her waist. "Maybe that's part of what makes it so hard not to."

His dark green eyes searched hers, probing them,

holding them, and even though Kira knew she should pull away, even though she reminded herself of her vow that if he ever tried to kiss her again she would put a stop to it before it happened, she didn't pull away. And she didn't do anything to stop him from kissing her again.

In fact, somehow her palms were pressed to the hard wall of his chest and when he leaned forward, toward her, she did the same until their lips met.

And lingered this time.

Long enough for Kira to savor the heat of his mouth over hers. Long enough for her to kiss him back the way she'd been wishing she had the night before.

It was still only a soft kiss. A starter kiss. With lips just slightly parted. With eyes drifting closed. With the gentle brush of his breath against her cheek and the scent of his aftershave tantalizing her.

But it was kiss enough to make Kira's knees go weak. To wipe away every thought about why they shouldn't be doing it and wonder where it was going to go from there.

That thought gave her a jolt. *Where was it going to go from there?*

It couldn't go anywhere from there. It shouldn't even be there.

It was just that it was so nice...

Then it was over, and she wasn't sure whether she'd ended it or he had. She only knew that, in spite of everything, she wished it hadn't ended.

Still, on the chance that she'd been the one to initiate the break, she tried to make light of it by saying, "Maybe you're just in too much pain to think straight."

Once more he smiled a leisurely, devilish smile. "Actually, I feel pretty good."

But he didn't try to kiss her again, and when she eased out of his grip he let her go.

"You're not supposed to be on that ankle," she reminded.

"I'll survive," he said, staying where he was, watching her.

"It must be getting late," she said then, afraid of what she might do if she didn't retreat. "And I don't suppose the girls sleep in even on Sunday."

"No, they don't."

"So we better rest up for the next onslaught."

Cutty just nodded his handsome head, his eyes never leaving her.

"Is there anything special going on tomorrow? Do you go to church?"

"The girls in church? That's just asking for disaster. I do usually barbecue on Sunday, though. It might take a joint effort, but I think I can stand long enough for that—if you're game."

It was a nice thought—a Sunday at home with a family, Cutty barbecuing, maybe eating outside. So much better than the Sundays Kira frequently spent— long, boring days that ended with solitary TV dinners.

"Barbecuing sounds good," she said. Then, before the urge to kiss him again became any stronger and caused her to actually act on it, she said, "I'll see you in the morning then."

Another nod. "'Night," he said in a husky whisper that only made her want to stay all the more.

And the fact that she *did* want to stay was her cue to go...while she still could.

"Good night," she responded, wasting not even another moment before she forced herself to go out the back door.

But all she really wanted to do was to stay right there in that kitchen with him. With his arms wrapped around her waist the way they'd been. With his mouth against hers and hers against his.

Exploring every possibility of where they might go from there after all!

Chapter Five

"Hi, Kit, it's me," Kira said into her cell phone at 6:45 the next morning when her best friend answered her call.

"I know it's you, your number showed on my caller ID, or I wouldn't have answered," Kit Mac-Intyre said.

"Because you're up to your elbows in frosting for the cake for the Blumberg wedding. I knew you had to start working on it at dawn this morning so I was safe calling you this early."

"You're almost right. I'm up to my elbows in ganache," Kit corrected. "But I should have the cake finished in time to deliver it by three and still be able to pick you up at the airport at four."

"There's been a change of plans," Kira informed

her. But before she got into that she said, "How was your trip?"

Kit had left Denver the same day Kira had to go to her great-great-aunt's funeral in Iowa.

"It wasn't too bad. As far as that kind of thing goes. My aunt was ninety-six and she outlived so many people that it was a small, quiet send-off. Mostly I'm just kind of bleary-eyed. I didn't get in until one this morning, and I had to be up at five to work on this cake. How about your trip? Why the change of plans?" Kit asked.

Kira had met Kit two years ago when Kira had moved into the apartment across the hall from her. For the first three months that they'd been neighbors they'd only exchanged enough information for Kit to know that Kira was working on her doctorate degree in microbiology, and for Kira to learn that Kit was the Kit of Kit's Cakes—a well-known Denver shop that specialized in special-occasion cakes—primarily for weddings.

But during a snowstorm that had stranded them without electricity for a full weekend they'd shared blankets, candles, food and the stories of their lives, and come out of the experience friends. Kit was the only close friend Kira had had since Marla had left home.

By now Kit knew everything there was to know about Kira, including what had taken her to Montana. What Kit didn't know—since they'd gone in opposite directions on Wednesday and hadn't been able to talk—was what Kira had discovered in Montana.

So Kira told her friend that her worst fears had proven true, that, yes, the Cutler Grant in the article was the Cutler Grant who had eloped with her sister, but that Marla and Anthony had been killed.

"I'm so sorry," Kit said. "I know you were hoping you would find Marla and your nephew, and have a family again. Are you okay?"

"I am. I have some sad times every now and then, but I guess in a lot of ways I mourned the loss of Marla when she left thirteen years ago. And as for having a family again—there are still the twins."

"So they *are* your nieces?"

"They are."

"Tell me about them," Kit urged in a lighter tone. "Are they cute?"

"They're so cute you just wouldn't believe it. But they're so busy you wouldn't believe that, either. They're into everything. They climb like monkeys— if I so much as leave a kitchen chair a few inches from being pushed in they'll be dancing on the table or dumping breakfast cereal all over it and spilling milk and juice into the mix."

Kit laughed. "Are they identical, or can you tell them apart?"

"They look just alike—they both have curly brown hair and big green eyes and cheeks so chubby you just want to kiss them. But one of them has a tiny mole the other one doesn't and I can usually tell them apart by the differences in their personalities. Mel— that's short for Melanie—is all girl, while Mandy seems to have a touch of tomboy in her. She's more adventurous, braver. Mel can be on the timid side, but she loves looking at herself in the mirror. She makes faces and preens—it's hilarious.''

''Do they walk? Talk?''

''They say a few words. *No* is their favorite—it's the first thing they say to everything. They do walk and would rather do that than be carried and—believe me—they get around. It's a full-time job just chasing them. They would also rather feed themselves than be fed, but they don't get much into their mouths so someone has to help. And whatever one of them does, the other one imitates.''

''They sound like so much fun,'' Kit said. ''Make sure you bring home pictures.''

Kira was surprised by the twinge that came out of nowhere at the thought of going home and leaving the twins behind. And Cutty.

But that was the last thing she wanted to think about now and she was glad when Kit provided a distraction by saying, ''So, let me guess—you're having such a good time with your nieces that you decided to spend a few more days with them?''

''Actually, when I got here the woman who usually works as the nanny and housekeeper needed some time off to care for her mother. So I talked Cutty into letting me stay to help him and get to know the girls in the process.''

''Does that mean *you're* the nanny and house-keeper?''

''That's what it means,'' Kira confirmed. ''Informally, anyway. I didn't know what I was going to do with myself until classes start and I just thought why not help out here?''

"I'll bet you've already taken a toothbrush to the bathroom tile, haven't you?''

"As a matter of fact I haven't cleaned the bathrooms hardly at all. You wouldn't believe how bad I am at juggling a house and kids, Kit.''

"You're not bad at anything. And you're especially not bad at cleaning—your apartment is nearly sterile.''

"No, honestly, I'm bad at this. I just can't get on top of things. I mean, I start every day with good intentions, but that's as far as it goes. I get the girls up in the morning and feed them breakfast. Then I pile the dirty dishes in the sink so I can take them upstairs to get them dressed and before I know it the day is over and all I've accomplished is chasing babies from one place—or from one catastrophe—to another, and I've left a trail of more dirty dishes and laundry and diapers and mess and chaos behind me.''

Kit laughed again. "I get the idea.''

"At first I thought it was because the twins didn't like me and it took so much to get them to cooperate. But now, even though I'm still not who they run to if they want comforting or something, they'll let me take care of them without a fight, and it still doesn't make any difference. Looking after babies ends up the only thing I really get done every single day.''

"That's something,'' her friend pointed out.

"But it's not enough.''

"Says who? The twins' dad?''

"Cutty? Oh, no, it isn't as if Cutty complains. He's great. Which is a problem in itself. Like last night, he talked me into going with him and the girls to a softball game when I should have stayed home and cleaned."

"Cutty is great?" Kit repeated, sounding intrigued by only that portion of Kira's statement.

"He's very nice," Kira amended.

"Is he very *nice looking?*" Kit fished.

"Yes, he's very nice looking."

"And you went to a baseball game with him last night?"

"Softball. It's this sort of informal league a bunch of the men around here belong to," Kira said, purposely expounding on the subject to get her friend off the track she'd been on. "You should have seen these guys, Kit. A few of them were average, but more of them were pretty amazing. It was like a whole bunch of calendar hunks all together at once. I kept getting introduced to one after another of them who were so gorgeous they nearly made my eyes pop out of their sockets. If you were in the market for a man I'd tell you to drop everything and come up here. It must be something in the Montana water."

"What about you? You could be in the market for a man."

Except that, as attractive as so many of the men she'd met the night before were, none of them had appealed to her as much as Cutty had.

But she didn't say that. She said, "Only I'm *not* in the market for a man."

Still, her friend saw through her. "Or maybe you've just already found one. In *Cutty*—whose name, by the way, you say reverently."

"Reverently?" Kira repeated. "You really do need sleep. You're hearing things. What I've found here is a ton of frustration and a challenge I can't measure up to." And she wasn't only talking about the kids and the housework.

"But you're determined to stay until you do—is that why there's been a change of plans?"

Kit said that with a note of innuendo in her voice, as if Cutty was the challenge. But Kira chose to take her friend's words at face value. "I don't know if I'll ever be able to do this as well as Marla did—or even come close—but I promised to help out until the regular lady—Betty—came back, so that's why there's been a change of plans. I switched my plane ticket to one that's open-ended, and I'll just play it by ear."

"Oh-oh," Kit said as if there was a problem with that.

"What's the matter?"

"You don't know if you'll ever be able to do as well as Marla did?" Kit said, paraphrasing that portion of Kira's statement. "Your father isn't there telling you you have to, is he?"

Kira laughed. "No. It's just that you should hear what people around here say about her. Everyone I've met goes on and on about how wonderful and amazing she was. The house was always immaculate. She never had a hair out of place. She was a pillar of the community. She was a saint with Anthony. She was devoted to him. She was…well, from all reports, she was—''

''You're killing yourself trying to be equally as good as your sister again, aren't you?'' Kit guessed.

''I wouldn't say I'm killing myself,'' Kira hedged.

''Oh, Kira,'' Kit said, sounding concerned.

''What?''

''Don't do to yourself what your father did to you for all that time.''

''I'm not.''

''No? Because it sure sounds like you are. He raised the bar higher than you—or anyone else—could ever reach and used Marla as the example of what you had to compete with to try, and, unless I'm hearing things, now you're doing the same thing.''

''*I'm* not using Marla as the example of the way things should be done, everyone else is.''

''And you're still trying to follow that example and feeling like you're not as good or as smart or as fantastic as you should be. Even though, chances are, Marla's greatness is being exaggerated all out of proportion.''

''I don't know, the Marla I knew *was* smart and beautiful and talented and great at everything. Do you think that when she got here she swept the dirt under the rugs or hid the unwashed dishes in the pantry and just fooled everybody?''

''I think,'' Kit said patiently, ''that Marla was *human*. I think she was human enough to sneak around to date a boy her father didn't want her to date and to get pregnant at seventeen. I think that even if her house was clean and she was a good mother, there were probably days when she didn't wash her hair or when the laundry was stacked somewhere out of sight. I think she wasn't some kind of wonder-woman and neither are you, and I hate seeing you falling into even more of a pattern of trying to be and finding fault with yourself for not making it."

"I don't have to find fault with myself, all I have to do is take one look at this house to know I'm failing," Kira said with a humorless laugh.

"See? *Failing*. You *aren't* failing. You're using your own vacation time to help out this guy. No matter what *doesn't* get done, that's still a really good, really generous thing to do. The twins are getting taken care of—which is the main thing, the thing that counts. But all you can say is how much you're *not* doing. From where I'm sitting, Cutty Grant is lucky to have you and should be grateful as all get-out."

"He's not *un*grateful," Kira said. "He's the one telling me to leave things until the next day or not to worry about what doesn't get done."

"Then maybe you should take *that* seriously and forget how stupendous Marla may or may not have been."

Easier said than done...

"Okay, I'll try," Kira said anyway, knowing her friend only wanted what was best for her.

"And in the meantime," Kit's tone turned sly, "maybe you can just enjoy your nieces and the very nice-looking *Cutty*."

Kit sounded like a dreamy-eyed teenager when she said Cutty's name and Kira laughed. "You are bad," she told her friend.

"Try it, you might like it," Kit advised with a lascivious intonation that made Kira laugh again.

"Bad, bad, bad. But will you use your key to my place to go in and water my plants until I get home?"

"You know I will. But only if you swear you'll let your hair down a little with Mr. Very Nice-Looking Montana Man. You deserve some fun, you know?"

"I know—all work and no play makes Kira a very dull girl," Kira repeated what Kit had said to her often since they'd met.

"Play is good for the metabolism—think of it that way," her friend added.

"I'll try," Kira said once more. "I'll also let you get back to your ganache so the Blumbergs can have cake at their reception today."

"Okay. Keep me posted," Kit said before they hung up.

But even as Kira turned off her phone she knew that, despite what she'd told her friend, she didn't need to try to have fun with Cutty. That happened all on its own.

What she did need to work at was trying to improve at everything else.

Because no matter what Kit thought, Kira knew deep down that she just had to be better at the job she'd taken on than she had been.

She just had to.

*　*　*

"Sim?"

"Sim?" Kira whispered back to Mandy, not understanding the word.

Kira had just gotten the girls up from their naps that afternoon, and Cutty was on the telephone in the kitchen where Kira had taken the twins and given them graham crackers to keep them occupied while she marinated the chicken Cutty was going to barbecue for dinner. But Mandy wasn't interested in the cracker. She was demanding whatever *sim* was.

And now that Mel had heard it, she obviously understood it and wanted it, too, because she began an excited chant, "Sim! Sim!"

"Shh!" Kira said in an attempt to keep the noise level down while Cutty was on the phone. Especially since the questions he was asking the caller were clearly police business. "Can you show me what you want?" she asked the girls as she covered the dish with the chicken and marinade in it and put it in the refrigerator.

"Sim!" Mandy demanded more forcefully now that she had her sister's support.

"I don't know what *sim* is," Kira informed the tiny child, unsure if either twin comprehended what she was trying to get through to them any more than she understood what they were telling her.

"Sim!" Mel shouted.

That prompted Cutty to say into the receiver, "Hang on a minute." Then, with his hand over the mouthpiece, he said to Kira, "*Sim* is swim. They want to swim in the blow-up pool in the backyard."

"Oh," Kira said as light dawned. "Should I let them?"

"It's up to you. You'll have to rinse out the pool, fill it from the hose, bring out a bucket of hot water to heat it and sit with them the whole time."

None of which involved making any headway on the chores Kira was hoping to get to.

Cutty must have seen her indecision because he said, "You can tell them no if you don't want to do it."

Then he went back to his phone conversation and left it up to her.

But by then Mandy had joined Mel in chanting, "Sim! Sim!" and Kira knew she'd be in for a raging tantrum in stereo if she told them they couldn't swim. So she caved.

"Okay, okay, we'll swim. For just a little while, though, because there are so many other things I need to get done today," she said to hush the girls.

"You can put them in the pool in their diapers," Cutty informed her, taking another break from his call as she ushered the twins into the backyard.

Filling the pool with the hose hadn't sounded like a problem, but with Mel and Mandy in tow it was hardly uncomplicated. They didn't have any conception of waiting until Kira had it ready for them. Or them ready for it. Instead, as she was turning on the hose, they got into the small vinyl wading pool, getting their clothes soiled with the dirt that had dried on the bottom from disuse.

"No, we have to rinse it out and fill it before you can get in," Kira told them, setting the hose down on the lawn and going to lift them out.

"Sim!" Mel protested.

"We need water in it to swim," Kira said, putting Mel on the grass and then turning to get Mandy out.

But while she was retrieving Mandy, Mel picked up the hose and aimed it at the pool, dousing Kira and Mandy both, and making Mandy cry.

"Oh, this is not good," Kira muttered to herself, before attempting to comfort Mandy and get the hose from Mel at the same time.

Once she had the hose she put it down again but kept her foot firmly on it as she set Mandy on the lawn beside her sister.

"Can you take off your clothes while I put the water in the pool?" she asked, hoping to distract them, knowing they could undress themselves if they wanted to because they often did it at moments when they weren't supposed to.

But of course they both said, "No."

"Okay, then just sit there while I fill the pool."

Another *no* was the answer to that, but Kira ignored it, snatched up the hose and took it to the pool.

She managed to rinse it and dump out the dingy water but as she finally began to fill it the girls returned.

"Sim!" Mel said.

By then Kira knew better than to expect any patience from them, so she put the hose between her knees to hold it still aimed at the pool and, with her hands free, she went to work taking off the twins' shirts and shorts.

It was not a graceful operation but luckily the pool was so small it didn't take much to put a few inches of water into it, and the girls had on only shorts and T-shirts over their diapers.

With both things accomplished, she took the hose with her to turn it off and by the time she'd done that, the babies had climbed into the water.

"Coad!" Mandy complained, getting right back out.

"I know it's cold. I'm going to get some water from inside to heat it up."

But she couldn't leave Mel in the water while she did that, so she again lifted the baby out of the pool, making her scream bloody murder because she didn't want to get out.

"Go find the ball. You can take it into the pool with you," Kira said, hoping to distract Mel.

But it was Mandy who found the ball—and threw it into the water from a safe distance away—while Mel merely tried to get back in herself.

So, keeping an eagle eye on Mandy but leaving her in the yard, Kira took Mel into the house with her.

She was glad to see that Cutty was no longer on the telephone. If he had been he certainly wouldn't have been able to hear his conversation over Mel's crying and demanding to *sim* again. Instead he'd already filled a bucket with hot water.

"Thanks," Kira said, pretending not to notice that

he was amused by the spectacle of her swimming-pool comedy of errors.

She took the screaming infant and the bucket back outside but she needed two hands to pour the warmer water into the pool. Which meant she had to put Mel down.

But the minute she did, Mel climbed in again.

Kira was afraid she might burn the baby, so she took her out.

Mel's feet no sooner hit the ground than she climbed in.

Kira took her out.

Mel climbed in.

So Kira took her out, took her to the farthest end of the yard, and then ran as fast as she could to pour the water in before Mel got back, too.

Kira could hear Cutty laughing from inside the house so she knew he was watching, but she was just glad she'd managed to get all the hot water in and do a quick test of the temperature before Mel climbed into that pool again.

Then Kira turned to Mandy who was stomping her bare feet into the puddle left when Kira had rinsed the pool initially.

"The water is warm now, Mandy. Do you want to swim?"

"No."

Of course not. And no amount of coaxing could get the other baby anywhere near the water her sister was happily romping in now.

Kira was slowly learning to pick her battles and

forcing Mandy to swim didn't seem like one she should wage. Besides, after all that, she was ready for a breather herself. So rather than saying any more, she took a lawn chair to the edge of the wading pool where she could sit and watch Mel and Mandy at once, and sat down.

"Can I put my feet in?" she asked Mel.

"Sim?" Mel responded in invitation.

"No, thank you. I'm too big to swim. But I'll put my feet in," she said, taking off her own sandals and rolling up her jeans so she could do just that.

"Toes," Mel said, pointing to Kira's.

"Toes," Kira confirmed.

That drew Mandy's interest and she came to the pool's edge, too, bending over to get a look at Kira's feet, as well.

Kira wiggled her toes for them and that made them laugh.

Then Mandy left, dragged one of the two infant-size lawn chairs to Kira's side and tried to do what Kira was doing—sit in the chair and dangle her feet over the edge of the pool.

Her judge of distance was off, though, and she was too far away. So Kira helped out by moving Mandy and her chair close enough for Mandy's pudgy feet to reach.

She promptly wiggled her toes, too, and it must have looked like more fun than Mel was having because she climbed out of the pool, clumsily maneuvered her own pint-size chair to Kira's other side and wasn't happy until she was doing exactly what Mandy and Kira were doing.

And there they sat, three girls soaking their feet on a hot summer's day, wiggling their toes, making trails through the water, kicking up a light splash just for the heck of it.

And that was when it struck Kira that somewhere along the way she'd turned a corner with her nieces.

That not only had they accepted her, they might even like her.

And nothing she could think of pleased her more.

"If you do that over here I can help," Cutty informed Kira when she came down the stairs carrying a basket of clean laundry to fold after getting the twins to sleep that night.

"I won't pass up that offer," she said, struggling not to let anything fall from the mountain that peaked well above the top of the basket.

Cutty was in his usual position on the couch with his foot propped on top of pillows on the coffee table so Kira put the basket in front of the sofa and joined him on the other side of it.

Oddly enough, sharing the simple chore seemed like a nice way to end the day. A day Kira had enjoyed even more after the realization that she'd made headway in the twins' affections.

"Can I say *I told you so* now?" Cutty asked as they worked.

"About what?"

"The girls. Didn't I tell you they'd warm up to you if you just gave them a little time?"

"You did."

"And now they're passing up their dear old dad like a dirty shirt," he pretended to complain.

"You could have read their bedtime story if you wanted to," Kira pointed out, believing he was referring to the fact that the twins had decreed that "Kiwa" do the honors tonight.

"No, they made their choice and it wasn't me."

"Mel even wanted to give me a good-night kiss," Kira bragged. "Then, not to be outdone, I got one out of Mandy, too."

"You're on the A-list now."

Kira just smiled, keeping to herself how good that made her feel. And at the same time trying not to take too much notice of Cutty.

He had on casual Sunday clothes—a pair of jeans and a simple navy-blue crew-neck T-shirt—but every time he reached for something to fold his carved biceps slid out from under the short sleeve and Kira's gaze kept getting stuck on how sexy that looked.

"You're very patient with the girls," he said then.

"Why does that seem to surprise you?"

"Well, for one, they're a handful."

"And for two?"

He didn't seem eager to answer that because there was a moment's pause before he said, "I guess it comes from the image I have of the way you and Marla were raised."

''The *image* you have? Didn't Marla talk about the way we were raised?''

''No, as a matter of fact, she didn't. I made certain assumptions based on my experience with your father, but she said I was wrong.''

''What assumptions did you make?'' Kira asked.

''To be blunt? That he was domineering. Demanding. Dictatorial. Controlling in the extreme. Really, that he was just plain mean and that he ran his household like boot camp. And even though Marla swore he was never violent, patience was definitely not what I figured anyone learned from him.''

''No, he wasn't violent—that part was true. But Marla denied the rest?'' It was Kira's turn to sound surprised.

''She said her father was a model parent. That at times he could be a little stern but that didn't make him any less great. That I'd only seen him one night when he'd been upset, and that he'd had good reason to be angry.''

''Oh.''

They'd finished folding the laundry and they piled it back in the basket. A lot of the things were baby clothes, and Kira couldn't go into the nursery to put them away while the girls were sleeping, so she took the basket into the foyer and left it at the foot of the stairs, wondering the whole time at her sister's description of their father.

Then she rejoined Cutty on the couch, sitting slightly sideways so she could face him.

''Are you sure Marla was talking about *our* father?'' Kira asked then, making a little joke. ''Because the father I had was a lot more like your description than what I would consider a model parent.''

''It was important to Marla to have a good face on things,'' Cutty said, sounding a little sad. But it was short-lived. ''So tell me what he was really like.''

Kira had the sense that Cutty's curiosity came from more than merely a desire to know about her childhood. But even so she didn't see why that curiosity couldn't be satisfied. In fact she didn't understand why Marla *hadn't* satisfied it.

''Boot camp—that pretty much hits the nail on the head,'' Kira confirmed what Cutty had said moments earlier. ''One of my earliest memories of Tom Wentworth is of this big man towering over me and yelling because I hadn't made my bed the minute I got out of it—and made it complete with the sheet folded just so over the top edge of the blanket, the pillow centered and the spread exactly the same distance from the floor all the way around.''

''And you were how old when your mother married him?''

''Three. I don't know how soon it was afterward that I was in trouble for not making the bed, but I don't think it was too terribly long a time. I do know that there were always high expectations of me and some of the things he made us do seemed unnecessary.''

''For instance?''

''Well, for instance, besides the specifications for how the bed had to be made, at night our clothes either had to go into the hamper or be folded in a pile at the foot of the mattress, and our shoes had to be side-by-side under the bed—far enough under to be out of the way, not so far that the heels couldn't be seen. And if the shoes weren't where they were supposed to be or weren't absolutely side-by-side, he would wake us up with a scream that would scare us to death and make us do it the way he wanted it."

"So you were afraid of him even if he didn't hit you?"

"Oh, yeah," Kira said emphatically but matter-of-factly and without feeling sorry for herself.

"I know I'd never seen anyone as petrified as Marla was about telling her father that she was pregnant," Cutty put in.

"And then you met him and understood."

"But there was no hitting?" Cutty reiterated as if he couldn't believe it.

"No, he never hit us. Although there were a few times when he'd flick our ears—which hurt a lot. But that was as far as any physical consequences went. It was more that there were average punishments that he'd take a step—or ten steps—further."

"Like?"

"Like we didn't just have dessert taken away, we wouldn't get a meal at all. Toys wouldn't just be off-limits for a while, he'd pack everything up and give it to charity, and we wouldn't have anything to play with until the next Christmas or birthday. Extra chores didn't mean we had to sweep out the garage, it meant that we had to completely take the garage apart, scrub it down as if it were an operating room and put it back together. Extremes—he always did everything in the extreme. Including his reaction if we did step out of line or didn't perform to his standards. He could be very scary. And loud. If I disappointed him or made him mad I dreaded his reaction as much as I dreaded his punishments.''

''And your mother let this go on?''

''He was as hard on my mother as he was on Marla and me. He saw everything and everyone as a reflection of him, and that reflection had to be flawless. It was important that people marveled at how exceptional everything he had contact with was.''

''That's a lot of pressure.''

''A lot,'' Kira confirmed.

''And he was the same with your mother?''

''Dinner at six o'clock every night. If she served it at five after he was likely to throw it against a wall. She couldn't be seen without makeup. The house had to be spotless and everything had to be in exactly the order it had been before we moved in—the way his first wife had decorated it. Once he didn't speak to my mother for six months because she'd dusted the living room and moved a lamp to a spot she thought needed more light.''

''You're kidding?''

''I wish I were. The lamp was where Marla's mother had put it and that meant it couldn't be moved.''

''Was the place a shrine to his first wife?''

''To him it was more that his first wife had set the

standard my mother had to live by. Just the way Marla was the standard I was supposed to live by...well, in terms of getting straight As and minding my manners and being as good at everything as she was. At least as good as she'd been up to the point where she got pregnant.''

Cutty shook his head. ''I still can't believe your mother put up with it all—for herself or for you.''

Kira shrugged. ''He wasn't awful all the time. He could be nice. I think she genuinely loved him, even though I admit, I found him a hard man to love myself. But my mother always said that even though he ran a tight ship he was still a good man, that he provided for us and only wanted the best for us. Plus, she never thought she had a whole lot of options. She'd gotten married right out of high school, she didn't have a degree or any work experience, and when my birth father deserted us and disappeared so he didn't have to pay child support when I was a year old, she'd really been left in trouble. To her it was better to put up with Tom Wentworth's idiosyncrasies—that's what she called them—than to be on her own to raise and support me the way she'd been for the two years between her divorce and marrying again.''

Cutty's eyebrows came together in a frown. ''So did Wentworth ease up on you at least after Marla did the biggest no-no of all and got pregnant at seventeen?''

''Ease up?'' Kira repeated with a laugh. ''Oh, no. As a matter of fact, I sort of got punished for it.''

"*You* were punished because Marla got pregnant and eloped?"

"Not directly. But if you thought he was strict with Marla as a teenager, it was nothing compared to what he was with me."

"Did he lock you in a closet or make you wear a chastity belt?"

Kira laughed again. "It wasn't quite as bad as being locked in a closet or wearing medieval armor. But I wasn't allowed any social life. He made my mother take me to school and pick me up at the end of the day, and beyond that I couldn't go anywhere where either he or my mother wasn't supervising, and *never* either with a boy or if boys were being included."

"No boys—under any circumstances?"

"None. If a boy so much as called me about a school project I was in for it."

"Girlfriends only?"

"Right. And I didn't end up with many of those because the older I got, the more my friends wanted to do things without one of my parents having to go along and to be with boys, and since I couldn't—"

"You ended up without even girlfriends?"

"Basically. I mean, I'd see them at school, but—"

"Geez," Cutty said, cutting her off as if he couldn't listen to any more of what she was telling him despite the fact that she was still merely letting him know the way things had been without any sympathy seeking.

Then he said, "I knew what Marla and I did all those years ago had more repercussions than I could have ever imagined, but I never thought it hurt you. I suppose you didn't even get to go to a homecoming dance or a prom or anything."

"Nope. Not one. I couldn't be anywhere where any boy might get his hands on me," Kira confirmed.

Cutty didn't say anything for a moment. He just studied her face with that penetrating green gaze.

Then he reached a hand to the back of her neck, squeezing it gently and rubbing it with his thumb. "I'm so sorry. I hate that I made your life tougher than it had been before."

"It's okay. Who's to say I would have even been asked to a homecoming dance or a prom anyway?"

"Oh, you would have been asked. Believe me, you would have been asked," he said as if he knew something she didn't.

He was looking into her eyes and his hand had risen to caress the back of her head in a way that made just about everything seem better.

"I feel like I owe you a prom or something," he said in a quiet, husky tone.

"At least one," she joked, her own voice barely above an intimate whisper as she had a flashback of an old teenage fantasy of doing just that—of going to a prom with a guy so terrific looking that everyone there would be envious. Of dancing all evening with him gazing into her eyes alone—much the way Cutty was gazing into them right at that moment. Of being taken home afterward and being kissed good-night.

As if he knew what she was thinking, Cutty used that hand in her hair to pull her slowly nearer. Near enough to press his mouth to hers and actually give that good-night kiss the young Kira had longed for. So near that to keep from falling into him she had to turn more toward him, facing the back cushions, facing Cutty.

He kept that hand cradling her head but his other arm came around her, adding a dimension that hadn't been there in either of the kisses they'd shared before—holding her, bracing her, keeping her close as his lips parted over hers and deepened the kiss.

Kira answered in kind, letting her lips part, too, savoring the feel of that muscular arm across her back, of his hand doing that gentle massage.

Lips parted even more and his tongue came to say hello, testing the very edges of her teeth, taking a leisurely course to meet her tongue, tip to tip.

She didn't retreat from that, either. She welcomed it, welcomed the deepening of that kiss, following his lead circle for circle, being chased and giving chase.

He pulled her closer still, until she was half-way sitting on his lap, resting against the breadth of that massive chest.

She wrapped her arms around him, too, letting her palms ride the expanse of his shoulders, savoring the feel of all that strength and power. Savoring, too, the feel of her breasts against him as her nipples turned into hard knots and nudged at him.

No kiss she'd ever imagined and none she'd ever had before compared to that one. She lost herself in it, in the pure sensuality of it, the pure sensual pleasure of mouths opening ever wider, of tongues doing a passionate dance that was awakening things inside her that were hot and fiery, things that made her feel alive with needs, with desires, with hungers she didn't even know she had.

And she was a little afraid of that, of where letting herself get too carried away might lead.

And maybe Cutty sensed it. Or maybe he'd been struck by a similar thought, because at the same moment Kira began to ease out of that kiss, he did, too.

"Maybe we should call that one consolation for missing the prom," he suggested with a frustrated-sounding chuckle, as if every time he kissed her there needed to be an excuse.

"Want to hear about the math camp I had to miss?" she joked in response, as if he could compensate for that, too, while he was at it.

Cutty laughed, but he didn't kiss her again.

He also didn't let go of her, though. Instead he held her there. And she didn't try to move.

After another long moment of looking down into her eyes he finally said, "Tomorrow night North-bridge is giving Ad and me some kind of award—"

"For saving that family from the fire?"

"Mmm-hmm. Will you go with me?"

"To watch Mel and Mandy while you accept your award?"

"No, there's a teenage girl down the street who baby-sits for me here and there. I thought we could call her to stay with the twins and just you and I could go."

"Because I missed a few high-school dances?" she

asked, worrying slightly that he might be asking her out of guilt or pity or something after what she'd told him.

"No, not because you missed a few high-school dances," he said as if he didn't know where that had come from. "Because I'd like you to be there with me."

He said that as if he genuinely meant it, as if there couldn't possibly be any other reason, and it washed away that momentary fear born of her own self-doubt.

"I'd like to be there," she heard herself say, contrary to all the reasons she could think of *not* to.

"Then it's a date."

"Okay."

He kissed her again and it was in that moment that she realized their relationship had reached a new level. A more personal level.

A level that was different than where this had begun.

A level she'd never intended to reach.

Just then she sat up straighter, away from Cutty, to put an end to this evening.

"I'd better let you rest up for your big night tomorrow night, then," she said, wishing it hadn't come out sounding as if there was more than an awards ceremony that he needed to rest up for.

Cutty smiled a smile that let her know he'd heard it that way, too. "Uh-huh," he said with a healthy dose of innuendo. But then he let her off the hook. "I'll call Tiffy first thing in the morning to see if she can sit."

"Great," Kira said, getting to her feet. "I'll just see you tomorrow then."

Kira insisted he not get up and walk her to the door when he tried and instead hurried through the kitchen and outside to the backyard before she was tempted to take him up on the offer.

As much as she would have liked to have even a few more minutes with him, it just seemed too likely that if he walked her to the door it would put them in a position where he might kiss her again.

And the bottom line was that thought was just too appealing.

But she couldn't help regretting what she'd denied herself as she crossed the yard to the garage apartment.

Or wondering if maybe some of the self-restraint lessons she'd learned from her father did her more harm than good.

Chapter Six

"It's okay, Kira. It's not a big deal."

"It *is* a big deal. Betty told me how Marla kept the house. She told me how it was all supposed to be done. And now she'll come here and see that I still haven't managed to get on top of it."

"Kiwa wunnin'," Mel observed.

"Funny," Mandy contributed.

The twins had just gotten up from their Monday-afternoon naps. They were in their high chairs having crackers and milk, watching Kira rushing around the kitchen, frantically cleaning up.

Cutty had taken a call from Betty, who had said she had some free time and wanted to take the girls to the park. He'd encouraged her to come right over, thinking it would give Kira a break.

Then he'd hung up the phone, told Kira and all hell had broken loose.

Mel and Mandy seemed to find it very entertaining. Cutty didn't.

"A few dishes in the sink, some crumbs on the counter, toys on the living-room floor—don't worry about it. The place still looks better than it did before you got here."

"But not as good as when Marla took care of it, and I can't have Betty seeing a mess," Kira insisted.

Cutty shook his head. "It isn't a mess, it just looks lived-in. But if it would make you feel better, you can put the girls in their stroller out front, and I'll wait with them for Betty to get here. That way she won't even have to come in."

"That might seem rude," Kira fretted. "And what about when she brings them back? She'll want to come in then, I know it. And—"

"And by then you can get things straightened up, if it'll make you feel better. But she's not going to do a white-glove inspection. It'll be fine."

"It won't be the way Marla would have had it," Kira reiterated, more to herself than to him. But she did seem to be considering his suggestion. And once she had she said, "I suppose there's nothing else I can do."

Then she made a dash for the stroller.

"Finish your crackers, girls. Betty's coming to see you," Cutty informed his daughters, all the while keeping his eyes trained on the frenzied Kira.

The longer she was in Northbridge with him the

more he was realizing that there were two sides to her. There was this side of her—the side that worried she wasn't doing a good job, the side that never seemed to think she was accomplishing enough, the side that seemed in constant competition with Marla.

Then there was the other side. The side that was more inclined to roll with things. The side that worked harder at winning over the babies' affections than at cleaning the house. The side that paid attention to Mel and Mandy—and to Cutty—before she paid attention to dirty dishes or vacuuming floors.

That was the side Cutty knew he was a sucker for. Which was why he also knew it was the dangerous side. Because that was the softer side. The side that was fun. And sweet. And just a little bit quirky.

That was the side that kept causing him to lower his guard.

"Okay, I have the stroller out front, at the bottom of the steps and the diaper bag packed and ready," Kira announced when she bustled back into the kitchen a few minutes later, still operating at superspeed. "I'll put the girls in it and Betty can push them straight out of the yard as soon as she gets here."

Cutty didn't say anything to that. He just helped Mel finish her milk and wiped her face.

By the time he'd done that, Kira had cleaned up Mandy and taken her out of the high chair. Then she turned to lift Mel to the floor, too.

"I'll grab the sunblock and put it on them outside," Cutty said then.

"Oh, good, that will help."

Kira wasted no time herding the twins through the living room and out the front door.

Cutty watched her go, discouraged by the sight.

Then he grabbed his cane and the bottle of sunscreen and followed behind.

Kira had both twins in the stroller when he limped out onto the porch.

"You promise you won't let Betty inside?" she asked as he joined her.

"I promise."

"But you'll be nice about it so she won't get offended?"

"No, I'm going to tell her you've banned her from coming inside because you're an awful, unsociable person who's holding us hostage in a pigsty."

To Kira's credit she realized he was only being sarcastic and smiled. "Do that and I'll break your other ankle," she countered.

There was that dangerous side again, peeking out at him. And Cutty couldn't help grinning back at her. "In that case I guess I'll have to be nice about it."

"Thank you. Are you sure you'll be okay out here with the girls? It won't hurt your ankle not to have it elevated until Betty gets here?"

"I'll be fine."

But he still kept an eye on Kira as she went back into the house, thinking that witnessing that panic over someone finding a few things out of place was something he should brand on his brain.

He was having more and more trouble keeping in mind that this other side of her existed and it wasn't something he wanted to forget. It was something he needed *not* to forget.

Because, yes, she could pause in her panic and respond to his joke. Yes, she'd stopped long enough to think of him and make sure his waiting on the porch wouldn't cause him pain. But even if there was a part of her that had escaped the effects of having been raised by Tom Wentworth, there was still that other part of her that hadn't. And Cutty knew from experience that that part was nothing to ignore.

He settled himself to sit on the bottom step with the twins directly in front of him and his bum leg extended out to the side of the stroller.

As he slathered the twins with sunscreen he thought about all Kira had told him the night before about her father. He thought about how much it explained for him. But even so, understanding the root cause of something didn't mean that what grew from that root cause didn't exist. It didn't lessen the reality of living with what grew from that root cause. And he knew he had to keep that in mind.

It was just that when it came to Kira, he seemed to have a blind spot. A really big blind spot.

It was difficult not to. Especially when the Tom-Wentworth-influenced side of her was beneath the surface. Pretty far beneath it. And the surface was so damn appealing.

Not just because she was beautiful, either. Although she was. Every time he looked into those big blue eyes of hers it was like staring at a clear sky on a lazy summer afternoon. He loved the way her hair glistened in the sun, the way it fell to her shoulders when she left it loose. And there certainly wasn't a doubt that her body was great, that it was a body his hands itched to get hold of.

But the more he got to know her, the more things he found that he liked about her on top of the way she looked.

He didn't know how long it had been since he'd woken up every morning eager to face the day. He only knew it had been a long, long time.

But every single day Kira had been there had begun like that—he couldn't wait to see her. To hear her voice and everything she had to say. To smell the clean, fresh-flower scent of her. To learn what made her smile, what made her frown, what pleased her and what provoked her, what she liked and disliked. To watch those long-fingered hands at work and at play and wish for a moment when they might accidentally brush his skin. He couldn't wait to learn what she thought of something on the news or see the twins from her point of view, to laugh at them together. He just couldn't wait to be with her, to have meals with her, to tease her, to share every minute and every event with her.

And then what did he do when the day actually did get started? He willed it to pass so he could get to the end of the evening, when the twins were down for the night, and he could have that little bit of time alone with Kira.

As much as he looked forward to the day with her, he looked forward to the end of the day with her even more. He usually even had a contingency plan for how to get her to stay if she seemed inclined to go straight out to the garage apartment after the twins were in bed.

It was nice to sit and talk to her. She was easy to have a conversation with. Easy to confide in. And equally as easy to listen to. And then, of course, kissing her good-night had hardly been a chore.

Oh, yeah, he definitely had a blind spot when it came to Kira. A blind spot that lasted even after she left at night because he'd been going to bed regretting that the day and evening were over. Regretting that he was going to bed alone. And then lying in that lonely bed fantasizing about what it would be like if she were there with him. *Wanting* her there with him. Wishing he could just fall asleep so the morning would come quicker. Not being able to fall asleep at all for hours and hours because he couldn't stop thinking about her.

"Beh-ee!" Mandy announced, drawing Cutty out of his thoughts as the older woman parked her car at the curb just then.

Mel and Mandy got excited enough to stand up in the stroller and try to get out of it.

"Sit down or you can't go with Betty to the park," Cutty warned.

His longtime household helper turned off her engine and got out from behind the steering wheel, waving at the girls as she hurried up to kiss each of them in turn.

"Ooo, my little sweet-cheeks," she murmured affectionately to them both. "I've missed you."

"Beh-ee!" Mel shrieked while Mandy bounced gleefully in her seat.

Then Betty turned her attention to Cutty. "What are you doing out here? You're supposed to have that ankle elevated," she reprimanded.

"I know but I needed some fresh air so I thought I'd wait out here for you."

"How's it feeling?"

"Good," Cutty said.

"Is Marla's sister still here?"

Marla's sister.

Cutty never thought of Kira that way, and it occurred to him that maybe that was something else he should try, that it might narrow his blind spot.

"Kira is working inside, picking up after all of us," Cutty said. "She'll probably say hello when you get back."

"Pahk," Mandy demanded then, as if on cue, just when Cutty needed her to.

"I guess I'll *have* to see Kira when I get back," Betty said. "I can't keep these beauties waiting."

"They probably won't let you," Cutty agreed.

"Oh, I could just eat them up!" the older woman said, bending over to kiss their heads again.

Then she maneuvered the stroller so she could get between it and Cutty. "We'll only be an hour or so," she informed him as she pushed it down the walk.

"I put sunblock on them. The bottle's in the pouch if you need more," Cutty called after them.

"Go on into the house and get that ankle up," Betty ordered over her shoulder as she turned onto the sidewalk that ran in front of the house.

Cutty's ankle was beginning to throb so he knew that was exactly what he needed to do and got himself to his feet.

Marla's sister, he thought as he did to counteract the fact that he was also glad to be going inside because it meant he got to see Kira.

Marla's sister.

But as he lumbered up the steps to the porch he caught sight of Kira through the picture window. She was in the living room, dumping an armload of toys into the toy box in the corner and then straightening the knickknacks on the table nearby and bending to snatch up a T-shirt Mandy had spilled juice on earlier—all at a double-time pace.

Cutty sighed and shook his head, stopping to watch her without her realizing she had an audience, wondering if she had any idea that she was going overboard.

But as he looked on Kira hesitated suddenly. She glanced from the shirt to the entryway and back again.

Then she checked the time on the mantel clock.

Suddenly she crossed to the couch in a hurry, lifted one of the cushions and hid the shirt there, completely surprising him.

Cutty had to fight to keep from bursting out laughing.

And just that quick his blind spot was back in

place, and he had to wonder if he wasn't already in trouble with Kira Wentworth, regardless of whose sister she was.

The awards ceremony honoring Cutty and Ad that evening was held in the school auditorium. It was packed with a standing-room-only crowd as Cutty, Ad, Northbridge's mayor and the entire city council lined the stage behind a podium where a number of people spoke in praise of the two men and thanked them for the bravery that had saved an entire family. Even the dog Cutty and Ad had managed to free just before the beam had fallen and injured them both was in attendance.

The ceremony had a casual, friendly feel to it, and as Kira sat in the first row witnessing it all she was glad for Cutty. It pleased her that what he'd done with Ad—as well as everything else he did for the town— was recognized and appreciated. He really had found a home here and an extended family for himself.

At the end of the ceremony Ad was given his plaque first. His acceptance speech was brief and humorous but then turned more serious and heartfelt as he added his gratitude to Cutty for saving his life.

Kira didn't think there was a dry eye in the place as he openly voiced his affection and friendship and presented Cutty's plaque.

Cutty was obviously moved himself as he limped to the podium on his cane. The two men embraced roughly—the way men do—and then Cutty took over the microphone.

He stared down at the plaque for a long moment as if he was reading it, but Kira thought it was more likely he was getting his emotions under control. That opinion was supported when he had to clear his throat before he could speak.

"This is really nice," he began, unprepared but without any evidence of stage fright. He went on to give his own thanks for all that so many people in Northbridge had done for him over the years, for how much the small town and its citizens meant to him.

Kira listened intently, enjoying the chance to so freely study the impressive sight of the tall man with the broad, broad shoulders encased in a pale green shirt. He wore a tie tonight, a hunter-green tie that set off the color of his amazing eyes. He also had on dark slacks tailored to fall perfectly from his narrow hips, and even though he'd complimented Kira on her champagne-colored V-necked silk blouse and matching slacks, and how nice her hair looked falling free to her shoulders, she thought he was definitely nothing to be overlooked himself.

He didn't talk for long but he did surprise Kira by aiming the last of what he had to say at her.

He sought her out in the crowd with those striking eyes and said, "I also want to thank Kira Wentworth who showed up on my doorstep out of the blue last week and volunteered to use her vacation to chase the twins and wait on me. She's kind of a ray of sunshine in our house and I want her to know how much I appreciate all she's doing for us."

There was nothing inappropriate in his words but

there was a hint of intimacy in the smile he shot her way, making her blush with more than embarrassment at being brought to everyone's attention.

Luckily, though, Cutty ended his speech then and in the applause and cheers and standing ovation that followed, she hoped no one noticed the pink hue of her cheeks.

There was a dinner in the gymnasium afterward, and while a number of people made a point of talking to her and showing an interest in her, Cutty and Ad were the men of the hour and barely managed to eat in the midst of the many well-wishers who wanted to shake their hands.

It was nearly ten o'clock when the evening finally ended. Ad walked with Cutty and Kira out to the parking lot and as he did he said, "Tomorrow night's all set. My sister can't wait to get her hands on the twins."

Cutty made a face. "I was waiting to spring the party on Kira on the way home," he said pointedly to his friend.

"Tomorrow is our boy's birthday," Ad explained to Kira, ignoring Cutty's obvious reluctance to talk about this. "I'm closing down the restaurant for the night. My sister is keeping the twins at her place until the next morning, and I'm throwing him the biggest birthday bash he's ever seen."

"Tomorrow's your birthday?" Kira repeated, aiming the question at Cutty.

He made another face. "It's unavoidable."

"Yes, it is. Birthdays are a big deal and we're celebrating it. Kira included, right?'' Ad said, looking for confirmation from her.

Before she could answer Cutty said, "I was hoping she would come with me but I wanted to ask her in private."

"Oops," Ad said with an ornery grin.

They'd reached Cutty's car by then and Ad went on to his own where it was parked one spot over, saying as he did, "Tomorrow night. Eight o'clock. No excuses. Kira, you can bring your dancing shoes even if Cutty can't dance—there'll be music and food and plenty to drink."

They all said good-night then and Kira and Cutty got into Cutty's car.

"I'm sorry about that," he said before he'd even put the key in the ignition.

"That's okay. I wish I had known earlier that tomorrow is your birthday, though."

"I really don't like a fuss to be made about it. But now that Ad has blown my plan to ease you into the idea, would you like to go with me to a party tomorrow night?"

"What was your plan to ease me into the idea?" Kira asked rather than answering his question.

"I was going to see if you might like to take a drive tonight, show you the north bridge that inspired the town's name, and then spring it on you."

Kira laughed, thrilled more than he would ever know by the fact that he'd had a plan at all for prolonging this evening.

"I'd like to see the bridge," she said then.

"And the party tomorrow night?"

"I'll think about it until after I see the bridge," she said, as if there was any doubt she would accept an invitation to go with him to his own birthday party.

"Fair enough," he said, starting the engine and pulling out of the school parking lot.

"So there really is a north bridge?" Kira asked along the way.

"An old oak one. Built across the river north of town. Actually, the bridge is more impressive than the river—which isn't much more than a creek anymore."

They were outside the city limits within a few minutes but Cutty kept on driving along a dark country road.

They went about seven miles before he turned onto another road—this one more narrow and less developed than the other, following it through an area that grew more and more densely wooded until they finally came to a clearing.

The bridge was a short distance ahead when Cutty pulled to a stop. He turned off the engine and the car lights so they could see it in the moonlight.

It was indeed a wooden bridge with crosshatch bars running the length of both sides and a railing bracing posts that held a shingled roof over it.

"The only thing it's missing is a horse-drawn wagon clomping across it," Kira observed of the bridge that seemed right out of the pages of a history book.

"That was just what it was built for ninety-nine years ago. It gets its hundredth birthday next year."

"I saw a covered bridge similar to that on a trip to Vermont. Once upon a time," Kira said then.

Cutty angled her way and stretched an arm along the seat back, transferring his focus from the bridge to her. "What were you doing in Vermont?"

"Meeting the parents of a guy I was dating."

Despite the view of the old bridge, Kira went from looking at it to looking at Cutty because he was still a sight she preferred. And when she did she got to see his eyebrows arch.

"You dated a guy seriously enough to go across the country to meet his parents?"

"Why do you sound so surprised?"

Cutty shrugged. "I guess after hearing about how things were for you in the Wentworth household I just didn't imagine you involved with anyone."

"I did eventually move out of the Wentworth household, you know."

"When?"

"About two years ago. I stayed at home while I got my undergraduate and master's degrees, and you're right—I still couldn't really date as long as I was living under my father's roof. Although I did have a little more contact with the opposite sex because of the freedom and flexibility college offered. But beyond having coffee with a guy or lunch or dinner between classes, I couldn't have a relationship that involved much else."

"Even when you hit your twenties? Your father still wouldn't stand for you dating?"

"It wasn't as if there was a magic age at which he started to see me as a flesh-and-blood human being who was entitled to a life. That never happened. I had to *excel* so he looked good. That was all he thought about regardless of how old I was."

"But after you got your master's degree you moved out on your own?"

"I did."

"And your father was okay with that then?"

"He didn't speak to me for six months. I wasn't allowed to go to Christmas dinner that year."

"That sounds like the man I hardly knew and didn't love," Cutty said wryly.

"It wasn't as if he ever willingly relinquished control of anything or anyone, so my moving out wasn't something he could just roll with. But when the silent treatment didn't make me move back in, he eventually had to accept that I'd left and wasn't coming back. Plus it helped that he saw that even though I wasn't living with him, I was still working hard as a research assistant and getting my Ph.D.—which meant I was staying the course the way I was supposed to."

"So even though you were finally out from under his thumb you stayed regimented—you still didn't cut loose?"

Kira laughed. "I definitely didn't cut loose. I moved into the studio apartment I live in now, worked days at the lab and nights and weekends on my doctorate dissertation.''

"Then when did Mr. Vermont come into the picture?'' Cutty asked.

Did he sound a shade jealous?

Kira smiled at that possibility. *"Mr. Vermont* was my advisor for my master's thesis. As long as I was working on it we kept things impersonal, but when I finished it and we wouldn't be seeing each other again on a professional basis, he asked me out. Although I didn't call him *Mr. Vermont.* I called him Mark.''

"Mark,'' Cutty echoed only with a more distasteful inflection in his voice.

"Mark Myers,'' Kira elaborated, thinking Cutty really might be jealous. And loving it.

"And he was your first…boyfriend?''

"He wasn't the first guy who ever kissed me. There were a couple of stolen kisses that went with those secret lunches and dinners through undergrad and my master's program. But Mark was the first everything else.''

And the last. But Kira didn't add that.

"So if you went to Vermont to meet parents, does that mean you were really serious about him?''

"We were talking marriage,'' Kira confirmed. "Although I still hadn't been brave enough to tell my parents about him because I knew my father would hit the ceiling. He would have said I was letting someone interfere with my education, that I was going to end up throwing away my life—'' Kira cut herself short. "Well, you can probably guess what he would have said. But I was serious enough about Mark that I was on the verge of going through all that to have a future with him.''

''What happened?''

''I guess I met his parents,'' she said, trying to make a joke of something that hadn't held any humor for her.

''Was there something wrong with them?'' Cutty asked quietly, apparently sensing the more somber aspects that had returned to stab her even now.

''No, Mark's parents were great. It was just that once I met them things with Mark became a little too clear.''

''What kind of things?''

''Well, I'd always known that Mark thought highly of his mom and dad—his mother in particular. I thought it was nice and I was looking forward to being a part of a family that had good relationships with each other.''

''But the truth was they were as dysfunctional as the rest of us?'' Cutty said, making his own attempt to lighten the tone.

''No, they really were a picture-perfect family. It was just that I didn't know until that trip that Mark considered his mother the epitome of what any wife of his would have to be.''

''Mark Myers was a mama's boy,'' Cutty concluded.

''There was more to it than that. For me, at least. I spent my whole life watching my mother trying to live up to my father's first wife. And never making it. I hated that so much.''

Kira had to swallow back the anger that the mere memory could still rouse in her.

When she had she continued. ''Even though Mark wasn't as controlling as my father, there was still an image of someone else that he expected me to emulate. That he was *demanding* that I fashion myself and my whole life after. I had this vision of making pot roast after pot roast that wasn't as good as the pot roast his mother made, and I knew there was no way I was going to put myself in that position. Almost the same position my mother had been in.''

''So you broke it off with Mr. Vermont.''

''I just had to,'' Kira said, suddenly thinking of too many similarities between the situation with Mark and the situation she was in now.

''Well, for what it's worth, I'm glad you did,'' Cutty said then with a devilish smile that succeeded where his joke had failed to break some of the tension this conversation had caused.

''Why are you glad I broke up with him?'' Kira asked a bit coyly.

''Because if you hadn't you'd probably be so busy making pot roasts that you never would have come to Northbridge, and I'd have to go to my birthday party tomorrow night by myself.''

There was such a glint of mischief in his eyes that Kira could see it even in only moon glow and it made her smile. ''I haven't said that I *will* go to your birthday party tomorrow night.''

"You would turn down a man on his birthday?" Cutty said as if the very idea was unfathomable.

"Maybe I have a mean streak you haven't seen yet."

That just made him grin. "Let's see it then," he said as if he were asking to see something a whole lot more enticing.

He suddenly let his seat slide back as far as it would go and, as if she weighed nothing at all, he half lifted, half pulled her toward him so she found herself facing him and sitting partially on his lap.

Even after the fact Kira wasn't too sure how she'd gotten there but she didn't protest. Instead she played along and said, "I don't show it to just anyone on demand."

"Maybe I can coax it out of you," he suggested, running the tip of his nose along her cheek like the stroke of a sable paintbrush.

"I'm uncoaxable," Kira said in a breathy voice that made a liar out of her.

Not that she cared. She was too lost in thoughts of how much she liked being there with his arms draped around her and his nose tantalizing her.

She closed her eyes and reveled in the tingling, teasing sensation that traveled to the edge of her jawbone, to her earlobe, to the side of her neck where he replaced the whispery strokes of his nose with a kiss. A brief, delicate kiss heated by his breath, warming her from the inside out.

He kissed her chin then. And her bottom lip alone before he finally took her mouth with his. But only playfully. Lips met and separated. Met again. And again, staying only after that third kiss to make it a real one.

Cutty brought a hand to her face, cupping her cheek as he parted his lips and urged hers to follow, allowing tongues to come out and toy with each other.

Kira let her hand rise to the strong cord of his neck, to his hair where it bristled at his nape. In the slightly odd position she was in, her breasts were against the inside of his arm and she felt her nipples tighten there, greeting him all on their own.

For a moment she wondered if he could feel it, too. But her curiosity was short-lived because just then he flexed back at them in answer.

It was a small thing and yet it was enough to make her breasts come to life with a yearning for more than the feel of his muscled arm.

Cutty didn't hesitate to trail his hand from her face even as he went on kissing her, their mouths open wide by then. Firm fingers traced a path to her shoulder and downward until he cupped one breast.

The pleasure was instant and caught Kira's breath, expanding her lungs suddenly and pushing that nipple more deeply into his palm.

His hand closed around her engorged flesh and Kira was torn between how wonderful it felt and desperately wanting the feel of it without the filter of clothes.

Longing for any touch of skin, she untied his tie and pulled it free, then she went to work on the buttons of his shirt until she had them all unfastened so she could plunge her hands inside.

He was hot and smooth and hard muscled, and she suddenly became aware of the fact that there was an insistent ridge letting its presence be known at her hip.

A quiet moan rolled from Cutty's throat as his mouth deserted hers to kiss her neck again, to nibble her earlobe.

Kira let her head fall back to free the way to the hollow of her throat as his hand slipped beneath her silk blouse and coursed up under her lacy bra to envelop that breast that was straining for him.

Oh, but it felt wonderful! And if there had been anything left sleeping inside her before, it all awakened with that touch of his hand. Every nerve ending, every inch of her body was suddenly alive with wanting him.

She brought her mouth to his once again, in a kiss that was lush with need as she writhed beneath his wondrous hand. A need greater than anything she'd ever experienced before. A need to cast aside all inhibitions, all reason, all caution....

That wasn't like her and a part of her froze internally at just the thought.

Froze and then retreated to a safer place.

A place where she wasn't tempted to do anything she might regret.

And she heard herself say, "Maybe we should slow down."

Cutty didn't just slow down. He stopped. He

stopped nuzzling the soft underside of her jaw with his nose. He stopped kneading her breast and merely let his hand curve along her side. He stopped everything to look into her eyes.

"Okay," he said but with confusion in his tone.

"This has all happened fast and—" And she was stammering and flustered and not completely committed to really having this end when her body was still screaming for it to go on, even if her mind had taken a different direction.

"It's all right," Cutty assured her in a voice that was husky and sexy and just made her want to start all over again. "What are we going to do anyway?" he added, "Crawl into the back seat like two teenagers?"

Kira was tempted to shout *Okay, let's do that!*

But she didn't. In fact, she didn't even stay where she was. Without saying anything at all, she moved away from Cutty, back to the passenger side of the car.

She wasn't sure what had happened to his tie but he began to rebutton his shirt front and seeing those big hands at work—those big hands she'd had on her bare skin, on her bare breast, only moments before—was enough to make her mouth go dry.

"You kind of go to my head," she said then, softly, closing her eyes to keep from watching him.

Cutty laughed sardonically. "Like too much to drink?"

"Like *way* too much to drink. It's almost as if I'm

someone else. Someone I'm not sure I even know. And I forget everything and just get swept up and—''

"I know. Me, too."

There was such understanding, such compassion in his voice that Kira relaxed a little and opened her eyes again to look at him.

His shirt was buttoned once more and tucked into his waistband, and one wrist was slung over the steering wheel so he could angle her way.

"But maybe that's not a bad thing," he suggested then. "I know it feels good to me."

"Maybe too good."

He chuckled. "There's no such thing."

Kira didn't know whether she agreed with that or not. Yes, he made her feel good. Better than she'd ever felt before. But the thought of letting go as much as she'd wanted to let go a few moments earlier, had terrified her, too.

Cutty didn't seem to notice that she hadn't agreed or disagreed with him. He just started the car then and turned it around, heading away from the covered bridge back to the main road.

Neither of them said anything at all through the entire drive home but the silence that went with them wasn't a tense silence. It was a thoughtful silence. A silence that let what they'd just shared linger in the air.

Only when Cutty had pulled the car into the garage and turned off the engine once more did he let those green eyes settle on her again.

"You still haven't told me if you'll go to the party

with me tomorrow night,'' he said, sounding so normal it brought her the rest of the way back to herself.

Kira considered what he was asking her, knowing it would be wiser for her to stay home with the twins while he celebrated his birthday without her.

But then he'd be celebrating his birthday without her. And she'd just about exhausted her willpower for one night.

"I'd like to go to your party," she finally admitted.

Cutty smiled a megawatt smile. "Right answer," he said as if she'd just given him the only gift he wanted.

They got out of the car and went inside to hear the baby-sitter's report that Mel and Mandy had gone to bed without incident and not made a sound since. Then Cutty escorted the sitter outside, insisting that he watch her walk home.

While he did, Kira didn't wait for him. She slipped out the back door and went to the garage apartment because she was afraid of what might be rekindled if she didn't, if they actually said good-night.

But as she undressed and climbed into bed she couldn't help thinking about what had happened tonight.

And about what *hadn't* happened.

And even though she recalled feeling safer not releasing that part of her that had wanted to be uninhibited, that had wanted to throw reason and caution to the wind, that had wanted to make love with Cutty, she couldn't help wishing that just this once she hadn't done what kept her out of trouble.

That just this once she'd been brave enough to do what she wanted to do instead....

Chapter Seven

"Y oo-hoo!"

Kira jumped, startled by the sound of a voice coming through the front screen. She was down on her hands and knees in the hallway that ran alongside the stairs—easily visible through the open door so the visitor hadn't knocked or rung the doorbell, she'd just *yoo-hooed* to announce herself.

"Betty," Kira greeted in return as she got to her feet and went to the screen, pushing it open to let the older woman in. "I didn't know you were coming over," she added, trying to sound happier than she felt by the surprise appearance of the nanny and housekeeper she was filling in for.

Not that she didn't like Betty, it was just that Kira still didn't feel that the house was up to par and at that moment there was even more clutter than usual due to the latest catastrophe.

"I couldn't let Cutty's birthday pass without baking him Marla's special cake," the older woman said once she was inside, holding up the cake container she was carrying and glancing into the living room in search of him.

When she didn't see him, she said in a more confidential tone, "I know this is the second birthday he's had without her and it won't be as hard as the first one was, but still I wanted to bring him a little of her anyway."

It struck Kira that every time it seemed as if the shadow of Marla might be receding just a tad, something—or someone—cropped up to expand it again.

"Cutty is out in the backyard on the lounger keeping an eye on the twins while I pick up this glass," Kira informed the other woman with a nod at the debris just behind her.

What had been a crystal vase on the small hall table was now in pieces all over the hardwood floor.

Mention of it drew Betty's attention to it and she let out a mournful wail. "Oh, no, that isn't Marla's favorite vase, is it?"

"If the vase that sits on this little table was her favorite then I'm afraid that's what it is."

"She loved that vase. And look at that gash in the floor—Marla worked so hard refinishing it. She would just be crushed to see that. What on earth happened?"

"Mandy threw a toy right at the vase and I lunged to try to block it and hit it myself," Kira confessed, feeling more guilty now that she had to answer to Betty than she had with Cutty who had merely said accidents happen and offered to take the girls out of harm's way while she cleaned up.

"I warned Marla that the vase might not be safe there but she said that was the perfect place for it, so it had to go there. And she was always so careful and so diligent that she proved me wrong and nothing ever did happen to it. Even when Anthony was in a fit, she didn't let things get out of control enough down here for anything to get broken. She would be heartsick."

Kira wasn't sure if she should apologize to Betty in lieu of Marla or not. She only knew that, even though the older woman was just talking and not trying to make her feel inept and clumsy in comparison to Marla, that was still what she accomplished.

"Maybe I can replace it," Kira offered.

"I'm sure you couldn't. Marla got it in an antique shop. Like so many of her pretty things. She had an eye for finding the only gem in a pile of rocks. That's why I'm always so careful around here—you can't just go out and find replacements."

Kira hoped Betty wouldn't realize that there was also one less glass banana in the decorative bowl of fruit Marla had kept on the counter in the kitchen. Kira had broken that the day before and she didn't want the other woman to think she was some kind of wrecker's ball going through Marla's house, destroying Marla's irreplaceable things.

"Why don't you go on out back with Cutty and

the girls?" Kira suggested then. "I'll pick this up and bring some dishes so we can all have a piece of your cake."

"It's Marla's cake. I can't take credit for the recipe."

"I can't wait to taste it."

"You'll love it. Everybody does. It won first prize at the County Fair three years ago and even got honorable mention in a national contest she entered. That girl could have been a pastry chef."

"I'm sure," Kira agreed as Betty stepped over the broken glass with a sad glance at it and headed for the back of the house.

Kira got down on all fours again to finish gathering the largest pieces of the vase. Of Marla's vase. Of Marla's favorite vase.

Marla's house. Marla's things.

As if she needed Betty to remind her.

Although, there were times when she lost sight of how she measured up to Marla, she realized. Like when she was playing with the twins.

Or alone with Cutty.

Of course some of those times were getting her into trouble, she also pointed out to herself. Those times when she ended up in Cutty's arms.

Or maybe what was happening was that she was finally doing a little of that cutting loose that Cutty had talked about the night before.

That was an interesting possibility.

Maybe she was doing a little of the cutting loose

she'd never done, not even when she'd moved out on her own. Not even with Mark Myers.

It was kind of an intriguing thought.

Cutting loose.

The more she considered it, the more she liked the idea. The more she liked the image that she was even *capable* of cutting loose.

Kira Wentworth, who had always done what was demanded of her, what was expected of her, who had never strayed from the straight and narrow, cutting loose...

Hmm.

"Cake, Ki-wa!"

That call came from the back-door screen to pull her out of her thoughts.

Kira recognized Mandy's voice and it made her smile. "I'll be right there," she called in return.

With the bigger pieces of glass gathered, she stood and took them to the trash, bringing a broom to the hallway to quickly sweep up what remained.

"Ki-wa? Cake!"

That one was Mel and this time Kira couldn't help laughing at the girls and their impatience.

"I'm coming," she said a bit distractedly as her thoughts went on wandering to this new notion of cutting loose.

Maybe even having come to Northbridge on the spur of the moment, staying when she hadn't had plans to, had both been a form of it for her. Baby steps, admittedly. But still it was certainly something her father wouldn't have condoned, and yet she'd done it anyway.

And look at what that had gotten her—Mel's and Mandy's affections and the beginnings of a relationship with them.

Which seemed to be an example of good occasionally coming from veering off the beaten path.

Another intriguing idea.

And if good could occasionally come from veering off the beaten path, from cutting loose, then maybe cutting loose—just a little—with Cutty wasn't such a crime, either.

It certainly didn't *feel* like a crime....

"Cake! Nee cake now, Ki-wa!"

Mel again.

"Just one minute," she said as if that meant anything at all to an eighteen-month-old.

She made sure nothing dangerous to the girls remained in the hall, then hurried to put away the broom and dustpan before she gathered plates, utensils and a knife to cut the cake.

And that was when she realized something else.

She realized that even just thinking of herself as capable of cutting loose gave her a new sense of daring.

Or was she just looking for an excuse to lower some of the barriers she kept telling herself she needed to maintain with Cutty?

It didn't feel nearly as nice to think that.

So she decided on the spot not to.

No, this was just a new dimension of herself. One

she liked. One that was probably long overdue. And she wasn't going to question it. Instead, she was going to accept it. Maybe even embrace it.

"Peez?" Mandy called, trying to lure Kira out with good manners.

But it was so sweet Kira couldn't resist it.

"Here I come," she said, leaving that last doubt behind her as she pushed the screen open with her rear end to join the small group in the yard.

"Cake, Ki-wa! Cake!" Mandy chanted as Mel charged Kira gleefully and hugged her leg in a bubbling-over of excitement.

Kira laughed and let herself revel in the pure joy of those babies. "Yes, we'll have cake," she promised. "But you have to let me get to the table to cut it."

That was enough to send both Mel and Mandy toddling for the picnic table where Cutty was now sitting lengthwise on one of the benches to keep his ankle propped up.

Betty took the top off the cake saver, revealing layers of yellow cake sandwiching whipped cream and raspberries, and topped with a chocolate glaze that dripped artistically down the sides.

"Betty has some news," Cutty said as Kira joined them.

There was something in his tone that Kira couldn't pinpoint but he didn't exactly sound happy.

"Everything's okay with your mother's back, isn't it?" Kira asked as she handed over the knife so the other woman could cut the cake.

"Better than okay," Betty said. "The injection they gave her has given her enough relief to start moving more, and her sister is coming to stay so I can get back to work around here."

Kira's heart sank and that new lease on life she'd been feeling in the house moments earlier threatened to go with it.

She didn't know what to say. She was there to help out while Betty couldn't, but if Betty's hiatus was over...

"Cutty said there was no hurry, that you have everything under control," Betty was saying, "but I just miss these darlings so much it hurts. And if you don't need to get back to Denver, maybe you and I can get to know each other."

Through her shock, Kira finally managed to think of a question. "When exactly will you be back?"

"My aunt should get in around noon tomorrow so I can probably be here after lunch."

"You don't want to spend some time with your aunt?" Kira asked.

"She'll probably be here a month or better so I'll see plenty of her. Besides, those first few hours she's here, she and my mother will be catching up and they won't even know I'm gone."

"Oh. That's nice then," Kira said, trying hard to mean it.

When what she was feeling was that the window of opportunity for more of that cutting loose just might be closing....

* * *

Ad's bar and restaurant looked like an Old English pub inside. The lighting was dim, the walls were paneled in dark wood and the bar was a long stretch of carved walnut with a brass foot rail along the bottom and a beveled-glass mirror behind it.

For the occasion of Cutty's birthday party that night the place that could accommodate a hundred and fifty patrons was well over capacity. All with Cutty at the center of attention where he sat on one chair at a corner table with his broken ankle propped on another chair.

A four-man band was playing live music on the stage at the opposite corner; there was dancing and a huge buffet, a birthday cake waiting to be cut, and even though Cutty was only drinking ginger ale because he was still taking antibiotics to keep the gash in his leg from getting infected, he seemed to be thoroughly enjoying himself.

Kira was enjoying herself, too. Although after two hours of so many people wanting to meet Marla's sister and regale her with more of Marla's accolades, she needed just a few minutes' breather.

She told Cutty she was going for a glass of water and made her way through the crowd. Only rather than asking the already overworked bartender, she went through the swinging doors next to the bar into the restaurant's deserted, brightly lit and much, much quieter kitchen.

Alone in there, she slipped her right foot out of the pointy-toed black mule that went with the dress she'd bought on a quick run to the local boutique while the twins were napping that afternoon. The dress was comfortable—it was a lightweight black-knit ankle-length A-line with a boat neck that looked deceptively prim in front but opened in a wide, low V in back. But the shoes were another story.

Kira arched her foot and wiggled her toes, and when she thought she could stand it again, she put her foot back in that shoe and gave her left one a reprieve, too.

Then she went to the sink and actually did refill her wineglass with water. But once she had she wasn't eager to rush back to the noise and commotion of the party and so she turned around and leaned her hips against the sink's edge to drink her water and enjoy a few more minutes of peace and quiet.

It was only a few minutes, though, before one of the swinging doors opened and in came Ad with a bowl that held only the remnants of potato salad.

He was startled to discover her and stopped short when he did.

Then he smiled and said, "Are you hiding in here?"

"No," Kira denied in a hurry. Then she smiled, too, because she liked Ad and admitted, "Well, maybe a little."

"It's wild out there," he said as if he understood her need for some escape.

"I've never been to a birthday party this big."

"Small town, big parties—it's hard not to invite just about everyone."

"And they all came," Kira marveled.

"Most of them," Ad said as he set the bowl down on a worktable in the center of the room and opened an industrial refrigerator to take out a container of potato salad.

He brought the container to the worktable and began to refill the bowl. "I expected a big turnout," he said. "This is the first time we've really been able to celebrate Cutty's birthday. Or anything else with him. Not many people would have missed it."

"Why is this the first time you've been able to celebrate anything with him?" Kira asked.

"Marla would never have come to something like this. Cutty wouldn't have come without her, so no parties," Ad finished matter-of-factly.

"Why wouldn't Marla have come?"

"It wouldn't have been a place for Anthony, and she wouldn't have left him home with a sitter."

"Ever?"

"She was pretty adamant about being the one to take care of him. She left him with Cutty of course. But no one else."

"Wow. She really was devoted to him," Kira remarked.

Ad didn't say anything to that. He also didn't seem to want to look Kira in the eye and instead became very interested in the potato salad.

For some reason it made Kira suspicious. "Wasn't she devoted to him? That's what Betty said."

"Sure she was."

There wasn't much conviction in that and it sparked a memory in Kira of the evening Ad had come to help with the twins while Cutty did the interview with the college-newspaper reporter. He'd started to say something that night and then cut himself off, saying he didn't want to tell tales out of school. Together with this now, it roused Kira's curiosity.

"Do you know something no one else does?" she joked.

Still, she expected him to say no. But instead he said, "Come on, this is a party. No serious talk."

So there *was* something serious to talk about?

"We're taking a break from the party, remember?" Kira said. "What do you know about my sister that no one else does?"

Ad frowned at her. "It's not like that."

"Then what is it like?"

"I just had a lot of time behind the scenes that other people didn't have, that's all."

"And were things different behind the scenes than they were on the stage?"

"You don't want to talk about this."

The more he tried not to, the more Kira *did* want to talk about it. So she pressed him. "Didn't you think as highly of Marla as Betty and everyone else around here seems to?"

"Marla was one of a kind," Ad said.

"That's the sort of thing that can either be a compliment or a criticism. Which is it?"

"I wouldn't criticize Marla. In a lot of ways she was a tortured soul."

"Because of Anthony?"

''There was more to it than that. Anthony was just one of the ways it came out.''

He didn't offer any explanation, though, and in order to encourage him Kira said, ''You know, I loved my sister but I didn't get to know her as an adult and from everything I've heard about her since I've been in Northbridge, she was too good to be true. I'd kind of like to know who she really was.''

Ad finished filling the bowl, closed the container and replaced it in the refrigerator. Then he returned to stand at the worktable across from Kira.

''How about if I just say Marla was driven and leave it at that?'' Ad suggested.

''A driven, tortured soul,'' Kira repeated. ''That's a lot different than anything else I've heard about her.''

Ad didn't comment one way or another.

Kira thought maybe if she opened up to him a little he might open up to her, so she said, ''You know, it hasn't been easy being Marla's younger sister. It's like she's always been just ahead of me, raising the bar. Even now, it's as if she's some kind of icon around here. I'd really just like to know the truth. Maybe to know she was only human, like the rest of us.''

Ad hadn't taken his eyes off her the entire time she'd been talking and Kira could tell she'd gotten through to him, that he was considering being honest with her.

But even when he did speak again he was still hedging.

"Marla was smart and talented and accomplished and good at just about everything."

"But…" Kira prompted with what seemed to be about to come after that.

Rather than continuing, though, Ad said, "Cutty wouldn't tell you this. He'd say it was all water under the bridge. That Marla's gone and none of it matters anymore. He sure as hell wouldn't say it to her *sister,* of all people."

"Then if you don't tell me I'll never know."

"You don't *need* to know," Ad reasoned.

But Kira thought that she did. For her own sake, because she was trying so hard to meet her sister's standards. And because she wanted to know everything she could about Cutty. About his past and what made him tick.

"I'd really like to know the truth," she said. "And I am family. It isn't as if you'd be gossiping."

Ad still wasn't eager to tell her what she wanted to know, and for a moment more he searched her face while he seemed to be deciding what to do.

But apparently her heartfelt, "Please," convinced him because he sighed and gave in.

"Marla was a very intense person. That didn't make her easy to live with. Not that Cutty complained, he didn't. I'm just saying that if I had been in his shoes, I couldn't have been married to Marla."

"Why not?"

"Everybody around here thought she was some kind of saint, or superwoman because that's what she tried to be. That's what she was determined to be. It was like a compulsion or something. She could never give up, she could never accept things the way they were, she could never stop trying to be the best at…'' Ad stopped as if he felt he was getting carried away. ''Let's just say that it didn't make for any kind of relaxed, balanced life. Not for her or for people who lived with her.''

''Believe it or not,'' Kira said to encourage him, ''I understand what you're saying. You could be describing Marla's father—my adoptive father.''

''So you know what it's like to live with.''

''Too well. My father was more rigid than anyone outside the house knew.''

''Rigid—that's a good way to put it. Marla was definitely rigid. And completely intolerant of even small things that went wrong. Or, for instance, something being half an inch out of place. She'd just go ballistic until everything was where she wanted it. *Exactly* where she wanted it.''

Which explained Betty, and even Ad, stressing that to her when they'd helped around the house, Kira thought.

''She also had schedules for everything,'' Ad continued. ''Schedules and routines that had to be followed or she just…exploded. And as for that *devotion* to Anthony?''

Ad cut himself short again suddenly, as if he'd said too much already.

''It's okay. This is important for me to know,'' Kira assured.

Still Ad hesitated. ''I don't want it to sound as if I

didn't like Marla. Really, it was just sad. It was really, really sad to watch someone push herself and everybody close to her the way she did. And when it came to Anthony—'' Ad shook his head. ''Well, Marla needed things—and people—to be unflawed.''

''And an autistic child is further away from that than a normal child,'' Kira guessed.

Ad nodded, looking as sad as he'd said the situation was. ''They didn't realize Anthony was autistic until he was about two,'' he continued. ''Before that it just seemed like he wasn't interested in the things babies can be entertained with or distracted by. He was just kind of unresponsive. But the doctor knew it wasn't right and that was when they figured out he was autistic. Marla came unglued when she heard that. She needed things to be perfect and Anthony wasn't. And after she went behind Cutty's back to call your father—''

''I didn't know she'd called him,'' Kira confessed, thinking that her call must have been the contact Cutty had said Marla had with the family after they'd eloped. ''I take it my father wasn't sympathetic?''

''He told her she'd gotten what she deserved. That Anthony being autistic was her punishment. And that he wouldn't have any part of it, nor would he do anything to help out. I believe the you-made-your-bed-now-lie-in-it card was the end of the conversation.''

Kira closed her eyes as her heart went out to the young Marla, imagining the desperation her sister must have felt.

"He was like that," Kira confirmed in a near whisper when she opened her eyes.

"After that," Ad went on, "Marla did what she did with everything—she tried harder. She tried desperately to make Anthony normal. To teach him. To control him. To get the autism out of him as if it were something that had possessed him and not just the way he was."

Ad paused, shook his head again, and then said, "I'm sorry. This is hardly a story to tell at a party."

"It's okay. I wanted to know." Then, thinking beyond all that Ad had told her, she said, "None of this could have been good for Cutty and Marla's marriage."

"No, it wasn't. Plus, it was a teenage, shotgun marriage as it was, and Marla's relationship with Cutty was the one thing she took for granted. The one thing she *didn't* work at. And even though Cutty tried to make it a real marriage—and he tried as hard at that as Marla tried for perfection in everything else—there just wasn't much there."

"So where did the twins come from?" Kira asked, not challenging what Ad was telling her, just confused.

"That was my doing."

Kira's eyes widened and Ad grimaced. "That didn't come out right. Here's the thing. I knew what Cutty went through trying to please Marla, trying to make the marriage a real one, and I also knew he needed a break himself. They'd never had a honeymoon or a single vacation, so for their anniversary I got together with friends—'' Ad pointed his chin in the direction from which the party was still going strong. ''A whole bunch of us pitched in, made the arrangements and gave them a trip to the Bahamas.''

''What about Anthony?''

''Marla didn't want to leave him, but with popular opinion urging her on, she also couldn't look ungrateful, so she conceded.''

''Who watched him?''

''He was familiar with my sister and me so we moved into the house with him to keep him in his same surroundings.''

''Did he do okay with that?''

''He was fine. But Marla wasn't. She and Cutty were supposed to be gone for seven days but she made him come home after two.''

''And the twins? You still haven't explained how you're responsible for them.''

''There was one night on the trip... That's where the twins came from. One night that ended up making the tension at home even worse and, even though Cutty never said it straight-out, my impression was that it was one night that proved to him that he didn't really have any marriage at all. That they were both just going through the motions. When they got back, Marla moved out of their bedroom into the guest room, and Cutty was sleeping on the couch from then until about six months ago when he got rid of the old bedroom furniture, bought new stuff and started to use the room again.''

''But they never considered divorce?'' Kira asked.

"Marla would have never admitted a failure like that, and Cutty would never have left her or Anthony," Ad said. "So they kept up the appearance of a happy marriage. An appearance that was helped along with Marla's pregnancy and having the twins. But underneath the surface, there was no substance."

Ad finished on a solemn note. He glanced in the direction of the party once more, but it was clear that only Cutty was on his mind and Kira thought he was worrying that his friend wouldn't have wanted him to say all he just had.

"He won't have to know unless you tell him yourself," Kira said, guessing what was going through Ad's mind.

But before Ad could confirm or deny it, one of the swinging doors opened and in popped Cutty's head.

"Hey, what're you two doing? The party's out here," he said jovially.

"You caught us," Ad joked. "I'm trying to steal her away."

"I knew that dress was going to knock 'em dead tonight," Cutty countered. Then he brought his cane through the opening of the doors and waved it like a weapon at Ad, laughing as he threatened, "Don't make me use this on you."

"My skull's already cracked," Ad joked in return.

"I'm headed for the facilities but when I get back I'd better see you filling out the ranks of this party," Cutty said then. "If I have to do this, so do the both of you," he added as if he wasn't having a good time when it was clear he was.

"On our way," Ad answered.

"You better be."

Cutty retreated and the doors swung shut after him, leaving Kira and Ad alone again.

Kira pushed off the sink's edge as Ad picked up the bowl of potato salad so they could follow him.

"Thanks for telling me all this," Kira said along the way.

They reached the doors and Ad raised a hand to one of them to push it open. But before he did he paused to look down at her.

"I might as well tell you one more thing while I'm at it," he said.

"There's more?"

"Only about Cutty. That big mug he just poked in here? I haven't seen it as happy as that until this last week you've been around. Call me silly, but I'm beginning to think it has something to do with you."

Ad pushed open the door and waited for her to go through it ahead of him.

Kira did, working to hide the fact that while everything he'd told her about Marla hadn't been as much of a shock to her as he might have thought it was, that last comment had really rocked her.

The party didn't end until after two in the morning, despite the fact that it was a Tuesday night. With the exception of Ad—who lived above the restaurant and also needed to lock up—Kira and Cutty were the last to leave after Cutty had said good-night to each of his guests and thanked Ad for everything.

The drive home was quick since the restaurant was only a few blocks from Cutty's house. Along the way Cutty and Kira talked about the wisdom in taking Ad's sister up on her offer to have the twins stay at her house for the night. They agreed they would have felt guilty if teenage Tiffy had been waiting this long for their return.

There was no one stirring on the block as they pulled into the driveway, and not so much as a light on in any house. Maybe that was why neither of them said anything as they got out of the car and walked up to the front door. Even as Cutty unlocked it and opened it for Kira they didn't disturb the silence of the sleeping night.

Only after the door was closed behind them did Cutty say, "I know it's late but I don't feel tired."

Kira didn't, either. Or maybe it was just that after a busy day and evening full of well-wishers, what she did feel was that she had barely seen Cutty and that she wanted to have that end-of-the-evening time alone with him in spite of how late that particular evening was ending.

"We're still probably wired from all that celebrating," she said. "But it *is* late," she added, just because it seemed as if she should.

"Yeah, I suppose it is. How about if I at least walk you all the way to your door tonight, though?"

"Your ankle isn't killing you?"

Cutty smiled a devilish smile she could only see in the moon glow that came through the glass in the upper half of the front door since they hadn't turned on a light. "I'm not feeling any pain at all," he assured.

"Magic ginger ale?"

"It must have been."

They went down the entry hall to the kitchen, not turning on a light there, either, and out the back door into the stillness of the backyard.

"So, did you have a good time?" Cutty asked as they crossed slowly to the garage apartment. "Or were you bored out of your mind being with so many people you didn't know?"

"I had a great time," Kira said, meaning it. "I haven't met anyone in Northbridge I haven't liked."

They reached the garage but Kira was still in no hurry to lose Cutty's company so even though she unlocked her door, she didn't open it or make any move to say good-night.

Cutty didn't, either. Instead he said, "What were you and Ad talking about when I found you in the kitchen? It seemed serious."

That was a question Kira had been hoping he wouldn't ask. But now that he had, she opted for being vague. "We were talking about you." Sort of. "You're really close—you and Ad—aren't you?"

"I never had a brother but I don't think I could be closer to one than I am to Ad."

"From what I've seen I'd say he feels the same about you," Kira said, hoping that was as far as the subject went.

It was, because Cutty seemed more interested in her than in talking about Ad as those green eyes did a slow roll downward and back up again. "You know, you look spectacular tonight," he said then.

"I wasn't ashamed to be seen with you, either," she countered, taking in the sight of him in a pair of charcoal-colored slacks and a black mock-turtleneck dress T-shirt that made him look far too dashing to be a small-town cop.

"I had two different guys grilling me about you," Cutty told her. "They both wanted to know if they could give you a call and ask you out while you're here."

"And what did you tell them?" Where did that coy, flirty tone of voice come from?

"I told them to keep their distance," he said in a way that left her wondering if he was kidding her.

"Would I have liked them?" she countered.

The devilishness quotient in his smile increased. "Not as well as you like me."

Kira laughed. "Who said I like you?"

He leaned over and whispered in her ear, "A little bird."

Then he tugged at her lobe with his teeth.

"You've been talking to birds?"

He straightened up and looked into her eyes. "They know a lot of things."

"Birds do?" she said skeptically, enjoying this game just because she was playing it with him.

"They fly around up there, watching us, listening to us. They see all and know all."

"But they eat worms so how can their judgement really be trusted?"

"Does that mean you *don't* like me?" he asked with enough of a bad-boy look in his eyes to let her know he was confident that wasn't the case.

"You never know," she said aloofly. "Could be I do. Could be I don't."

"Maybe I could win you over. If you don't."

"How?"

"How about like this?"

He leaned forward again, only this time he kissed her. A soft, simple kiss full of promise. A kiss that ended all too soon.

"Not bad," Kira judged when he drew back again. "But who knows? One of those other guys might have done better."

Cutty laughed. A low, sexy rumble of a laugh. "Guess I'll just have to try harder."

He propped his cane against the wall behind Kira, freeing both hands to hold her face on either side, his palms cupping her cheeks, his fingers in her hair as his mouth came to hers in a kiss much better, much more serious than the other one. A kiss that claimed her.

But it, too, ended after a few moments and he straightened away from her again.

"Well?" he said in a husky voice.

"Improving," she declared imperiously.

His laugh was sexier still. "I guess I'm on the right track then," he said before his mouth met hers once more.

No matter what she said, he was winning the game because her knees were getting weaker by the minute and she was having trouble not melting into that big body of his. Enough trouble so that she raised her palms to his chest to keep from giving in. Or at least to keep from giving in too easily. Plus it was nice to be touching that honed wall of muscle.

This time when he stopped kissing her he said, "Shall I call them tomorrow and give them the green light?"

With her eyes still closed she said, "Who?"

"The guys who want to ask you out," he answered with one more raspy chuckle before he recaptured her mouth, wrapping his arms around her to pull her close against him with those agile hands against her bare back where it was exposed by the V of her dress.

Oh, what the feel of his hands did to her! His skin pressed to hers was all it took to whisk her back in time to the previous evening. To reawaken everything inside her that he'd brought to life then.

Only tonight it didn't come with the fear of letting go. Tonight other things were racing through her mind.

Things like the fact that Betty would be taking over tomorrow and Kira didn't know where that would leave her. Or if she really would stay or go.

Things like the fact that she'd enjoyed the idea she'd fostered all day of cutting loose. Enjoyed that vision of herself. Enjoyed the possibility that she could.

Things like the fact that after she'd done what she'd thought she should do last night and not allowed this to go all the way to making love, she'd regretted it intensely. She'd gone to sleep wishing that just once she'd been brave enough to do what she wanted to do.

What she wanted to do right now.

Without breaking off their kiss, Kira reached behind her and found the doorknob, turning it and pushing the door open.

Cutty abandoned her lips to see what she'd done.

"Oh-oh," he said, clearly thinking she was going to leave him there.

But Kira picked up his cane and stepped over her threshold, taking it with her.

"You know that where the cane goes, I go," Cutty said with a wicked crook to one corner of his mouth.

"Is that so?" she said. Then she tossed the cane onto the bed.

Cutty laughed and his eyebrows rose. But he stayed in the doorway. "What about last night and moving too fast and—"

Kira answered him only by kicking off her shoes.

But it was enough for him to get the message, because he finally followed her inside, shutting the door behind him.

He still didn't actually come into the single room apartment, though. Instead he leaned back against the door, watching her through the moonlight that streamed in through the windows to provide the only illumination here, too.

"Tell me you know what you're doing," he said quietly.

"I'm doing just what I want," she said without

wavering because the longer she looked at him—at his sable-colored hair going every which way on top, at his ruggedly striking face, at that big body that seemed carved by an artist's hand—the more her whole being cried out for him.

"No doubts?" he asked.

"No doubts."

Still he stayed at the door, drinking in the sight of her just as she was him. Then he chuckled a little, took off his single shoe and sock, too, and came to where she waited beside the bed.

"This is really going to happen," he said as if that fact was just sinking in.

Kira only nodded, basking in his gaze as it seemed to savor her.

Then Cutty raised one hand to her upper arm and let it glide down to her wrist so he could bring that wrist to his lips to kiss the soft inner side, all the while holding her eyes with his.

His breath was warm against her skin. Sensuous. And she stepped nearer to close the small distance between them so he could kiss more than her wrist again.

Which was exactly what he did as his arms came around her once more. Only this time those hands of his delved into the sides of the open V of her dress, slipping up to her shoulders and moving forward to slide it off as his mouth opened over hers and his tongue came to pitch a little woo.

With very little encouragement her dress fell around her feet, leaving her only in her panties, and

Kira refused to be the only one of them without much on.

She wasted no time freeing his shirt from his slacks, interrupting the play of mouths and tongues to pull it off over his head.

With his chest bare, Cutty pulled her against him so her breasts could meet the hot silk of his pectorals as kisses turned urgent. Hungry. Demanding.

He didn't wait for her to deal with his pants. He took something from his pocket and then dropped them to join her dress on the floor before he divested her of her lacy thong, too.

He stopped kissing her then and searched her face, her eyes, as if to reassure himself she was real. And only after he seemed convinced did he reach around to set what he'd taken from his pocket on the night-stand so he could clasp her hands in his as he sat down on the mattress.

He left her standing a moment while he looked at her and a smile of appreciation lit his oh-so-handsome face, wiping away any self-consciousness Kira might have felt.

Then he pulled her to the bed, too. To lie on her back next to him as he lay on his side, their hands still together until he let hers go to brace his weight with one, to slip the other behind her head as his mouth found hers once again in a kiss of parted lips and tongues dueling in delight.

She raised her own hands to his head, to his hair—bristly and soft at once—and he caressed her face lovingly before trailing his hand down her neck, to the hollow of her throat, to her collarbone and shoulder.

He stopped there. But she didn't want him to. Not when her breasts were screaming for his touch.

She covered his hand with hers and urged it on, making him chuckle even as their mouths continued to cling.

Then to tease her he let only his fingertips trail a scant path, skimming just the surface of her skin, at a torturously snailish speed.

Kira groaned her complaint even as her tongue did a little pursuit of its own. But still Cutty took his time, letting those feathery fingertips glide all the way down the upper swell of her breast to her nipple.

Taut. Tight. That crest became a knot that greeted those fingertips and held its own as he took it gently between thumb and forefinger and tenderly rolled it back and forth.

Kira's groan became a moan when he finally took her breast into his palm, enclosing it in the warm strength of that hand she craved.

Kisses grew even hungrier. Even more urgent. Faster and freer, falling on lips and cheeks and chins.

Kira's hands filled themselves with his back— broad and strong and well muscled.

He was beside her and above her, his mouth a rain of kisses, his hand a miracle of kneading, of teasing, of tormenting, every movement of it raising her temperature, making her want him with an even greater intensity.

His mouth abandoned hers for good then, kissing

a leisurely route to her other breast, finding it first with his tongue to taunt that nipple, too.

Her back came off the mattress in response, leaving no doubt that she wanted more.

And more was what he gave.

He took her breast into the hot, wet darkness of his mouth, still using his talented tongue to toy with her nipple, circling it, flicking it, bringing it to life along with every other inch of her body.

Her own hands went traveling. Exploring. Seeking. Down the V of his back to the firm rise of that derriere she'd only glimpsed before that moment.

Lower, to the back of solid thighs.

Up again to his hips, giving him a bit of his own medicine when it came to tantalizing with anticipation.

It was Cutty's turn to groan and hers to laugh. But she granted his wish and let one hand course around to his front.

His moan was deeper and more gravelly than hers had been as she took him in hand, closing her fingers around that long, thick shaft of steel, reveling in the heat of him, the power, the potency.

But that seemed to be all he could take because he rolled away from her briefly, reaching for what he'd left on the nightstand.

"You came prepared?" Kira whispered.

"Just because of a hope-filled fantasy," he said, sheathing himself before he returned to rise above her, fitting himself between her thighs.

Thighs that Kira opened willingly, wanting nothing so much as to be completed by him.

He slid into her then as smoothly as if he had been carved from her. Filling her. Lowering his body to hers in a flawless joining of flesh.

He kissed her again then, easing himself more deeply into her, only to draw back and do it all again. And again until they were moving together too rapidly, too fiercely, for him to keep kissing her.

Kira just closed her eyes and let him carry her along, giving herself to him totally, relinquishing all control and allowing him to take her with him into sensations more incredible than anything she'd ever felt before.

Faster and faster, they moved as if their bodies had become one—in unison, in perfect rhythm. Striving. Straining. Working together until Kira felt as if she were no longer earthbound. As if she'd broken the ties of gravity to soar into the sky. Higher and higher until she burst through the clouds into a blindingly brilliant white bliss that stole her breath and left her cocooned in an eternal moment of unequaled ecstasy...

And then it retreated. Little by little they both came back to themselves. Muscles relaxed. Heavy breathing filled lungs with air again. And an exquisite calm settled them into each other's arms.

"Wow," Cutty said, sounding as awed as Kira felt.

"As good or not as good as your hope-filled fantasy?" she asked.

''The fantasy was surpassed a thousand times over. Are you okay?''

''*Okay* was surpassed a thousand times over, too.''

He smiled down at her and then buried his face in her tousled hair to kiss her head as he rolled them to their sides, keeping her close.

And that was how they stayed—his chin atop her head, his arm across her side, his leg over her hip— as total depletion of strength and energy overcame them.

Kira felt Cutty fall asleep but she didn't mind. It was just too nice to be there like that, with him, for her to care about anything.

Then she closed her own eyes, reveling in that moment, that afterglow, and all the warm feelings that went with it.

And when thoughts of what the next day might bring threatened to intrude she just pushed them away.

Chapter Eight

Cutty woke up the next morning in a haze of contentment, the likes of which he couldn't remember ever feeling before.

Without opening his eyes, he reached to the other side of the bed for Kira, expecting to find her there the way he had during the night when he'd drifted partially out of sleep and wanted to touch her or hold her.

But she wasn't there.

Even with his eyes closed he could tell morning light was all around him, so he thought she was probably in the bathroom and he let himself lie there, basking in that contentment that felt so damn good.

He knew he should probably get up. That Ad's sister would be bringing the twins home before long.

But still he stayed in that bed, enjoying the lingering memories of the remarkable night that had just passed. And the best birthday he'd ever had.

So this is what it's like to feel genuinely happy.

That was a bizarre thought to flash through his brain. Where had it come from?

Obviously from the way he was feeling. But still it struck him as odd.

Genuinely happy? Had he never been *genuinely* happy before?

Cutty rolled onto his back, eyes remaining closed, and began to dissect that possibility.

He didn't consider himself an *un*happy person. He made the best of what he had to work with. There were things he liked to do. Foods he liked to eat. Friends he liked spending time with. There were the twins. His job. Baseball, basketball, football games with the Northbridge Bruisers—he liked all of that.

But none of it had made him feel the way he did right at that moment. This was the kind of happiness he honestly didn't think he'd ever felt before.

He definitely hadn't felt it as a kid. There had been happy times, but a general, overall deep-rooted happiness? No, he couldn't say he'd felt that. Not while he was worrying about his dad and his dad's drinking, and how to cope with whatever came as a result of it.

Then there had been Marla.

Happiness wasn't something he thought of when he thought about Marla. Oh, sure, he'd been happy to hook up with her in high school. But like everything with Marla, even the start of the relationship had been complicated and so no, pure, unadulterated happiness was not the primary emotion he recalled.

Then she'd told him she was pregnant. That certainly hadn't made him happy. Neither had meeting Tom Wentworth or fighting with him or being in a position of having to elope. And happy wasn't how Cutty would describe having to come to Northbridge to live off the charity of his uncle.

Discovering that Anthony was autistic—there was no way *that* had been happy news. And the realities of living with Marla, of dealing with her relentless need for perfection. That hadn't put him in a state he would consider genuinely happy, either.

Even the birth of the twins had been marred by Marla's unhappiness at finding herself pregnant again. And what little marriage they'd had crumbling around his feet had been anything but happy.

And then there had been the accident. Losing Anthony and Marla. No matter how bad things had been at home before that, their deaths had struck a blow that he'd been struggling with ever since.

Still, it wasn't as if he'd had a miserable life, because he hadn't. It wasn't that he suffered from depression or anything like that. But when he thought about the course of things all strung together, he guessed he *could* say that he'd never really felt genuine, deep-rooted happiness.

The way he did now.

And it didn't take much to figure out why he felt that way now.

It was because of Kira.

It was as if she'd brought a light, a joy, into his life that had never been there before. He could relax with her as he'd never been able to relax with Marla. He could be himself without worrying that he was disappointing her somehow or letting her down. He just felt good when he was with her.

He felt happy.

Where was she, anyway? he wondered, finally opening his eyes.

Oh, yeah.

He wasn't in his own bed. He was in the bed in the garage apartment. He'd forgotten that.

It was the first time in ten years that he'd awakened there. And even though the place had been painted and the furniture was all new, even though it looked altogether different than it had when he and Marla and Anthony had lived there, finding himself there now was like being sucked backward in time. If Marla had charged out of the bathroom and screamed at him for laying around in bed, he wouldn't have been surprised.

And just that quick his sense of genuine happiness was tinged with an old familiar anxiousness.

Cutty sat up in bed, wanting to hang on to the good feelings, wanting to escape the not so good ones.

''Kira?'' he called.

Then it occurred to him that he hadn't heard a single sound come from the bathroom and that was the only place she could be where he wouldn't be able to see her.

So where was she?

Cutty glanced at the bedside clock for the first time and was shocked to find that it was already after ten. He hadn't thought it was *that* late. And Ad's sister had mentioned bringing the twins home around nine.

Had Kira heard the doorbell ring from out here?

He knew that wasn't likely.

But what *was* likely, he slowly began to think, was that Kira had left him in bed hours ago and gone across to the house to clean before Betty came this afternoon.

If memories of Marla hadn't totally deflated his joy moments earlier, that thought did the trick.

Cutty swung his legs over the side of the mattress.

His ankle shot pain up his leg in protest over the drop in altitude and he waited for it to ease up. Then he reached for the cane that was now propped against the nightstand rather than on the floor where it had rolled when he and Kira had joined it on the bed.

She must have picked it up and put it there. Just as it had to have been Kira who had neatly folded his pants and shirt on the nearby chair and so precisely situated his single shoe and sock immediately under it.

Thoughts of Marla again invaded at the sight of all that orderliness.

Thoughts about the similarities between Marla and Kira.

It left him all the more convinced of the reason Kira hadn't been there in bed with him when he woke up.

Damn.

Using the cane, he hooked his clothes and dragged them to him, his spirits deflating even further as he pictured Kira going through the house like a whirling dervish, cleaning and straightening and perfecting everything in her path. The same way Marla would have been.

He pulled on his shirt from the previous night, then his slacks and stood to bend over and grab his shoe and sock. But he didn't put them on. He just carried them with him out of the garage apartment.

And if what he'd felt when he first woke up had been a high high, trudging across the yard thinking that he was going to find Kira frantically whipping the house into shape to impress Betty was pretty close to a low low.

As he went in the back door he expected to hear the vacuum or water running, or something that would give him a clue as to where Kira was. But the house was quiet and he didn't find her anywhere on the first floor.

She's probably upstairs scrubbing down the walls or something, he thought as he made his way to the second level.

Again no sounds greeted him and in search of Kira and the twins, Cutty headed for the nursery.

The door was open and as he approached he finally spotted Kira.

She wasn't cleaning or folding clothes or any of what he'd assumed she'd be doing in anticipation of Betty, though. She was sitting cross-legged on the floor with Mel to her right and Mandy to her left, and they were putting the oversize pieces of a wooden puzzle together.

Intent on what they were doing, no one noticed him and Cutty stopped in his tracks. He'd been so sure he would find Kira in a panic to spruce up the place that seeing her like that actually shocked him.

Had she forgotten Betty was coming? That Betty would see the toys scattered in the living room? And laundry in the basket? And a baby handprint on the television screen?

He couldn't imagine that she had.

Yet there she was, playing with the twins rather than scurrying to make sure everything was impeccable.

Cutty stood there for a moment and watched the scene. Then, without letting Kira or his daughters know he was in the house, he went into his own room, closing the door quietly behind him.

"You jumped to that conclusion, didn't you, you jerk?" he muttered to himself.

But he really was a jerk, he thought, when one minute he was marveling at how terrific he felt all because of Kira and the next minute he was ready to condemn her.

And now here he was, wanting to hurry up and shower so he could be with her again.

"Maybe you should make up your mind," he advised himself as if he were talking to someone else.

He tossed his shoe into the closet, dropped his sock to the floor and stripped off his dress clothes to make a pile over the stocking. Then he headed for his bathroom.

But as he wrapped his cast to keep it dry and stepped into the shower, he started to consider that making-up-his-mind advice he'd just given himself.

He'd already recognized that there were two sides to Kira. That there was the side of her that was like Marla and the side of her that might have fretted over leaving the housework to go to the softball game but had gone anyway.

So if the side existed that could be persuaded to go to the softball game anyway—or sit and do a puzzle with the twins as she was right now—why had he been so quick to believe that it was the side like Marla that would prevail?

Standing under the shower's spray Cutty thought about it, trying to figure out whether he was being unfair to her.

He might be.

Because besides the softball game and finding her with the babies this morning, he also remembered this past Sunday when she'd set up the swimming pool in the backyard and ended up soaking her feet in the water with the twins rather than doing housework.

Plus there were a lot of times he recalled now that were smaller incidences of the same thing. Times when she'd read a story to the girls to distract them from mischief. Times when she'd patiently suffered the complications of one of the twins wanting to help her sweep the floor or dust the furniture. Times when a trip upstairs to do laundry had instead had Kira standing at the nursery door watching the babies sleep.

Times when the housework and laundry and dishes and other things left undone to vex that perfectionistic side of Kira had only been left undone *because* she was more likely to leave the chores in order to take care of him or the babies, to go with him when he asked her to, to play with Mel and Mandy....

That was a very big realization for him.

Big enough to cause him to pause for a minute to let it sink in.

And as it did, he had to admit that while, yes, there was a side of Kira that was like Marla, Marla had never had that other, softer, more flexible side that Kira had to balance it out.

Would Marla ever have left dishes in the sink or mud on the floor to go to a softball game with him?

Never.

Even during the brief month after Mel and Mandy were born, Marla had fed them, bathed them, dressed them and then handed them off to Betty to hold while she'd made sure no speck of dust was left to mar her sense of order.

So what did that mean? Cutty asked himself as he finished his shower, turned off the water and grabbed a towel to dry off.

For one thing, it meant that Kira was more fun.

And for another thing, it meant that she was easier to live with—even considering the fretting and the periodic mad dashes to clean.

That thought made him smile because it reminded

him of the day Betty had come to take the twins to the park, when Cutty had spotted Kira through the living-room window stashing that soiled baby shirt under the couch cushion. That was definitely not something Marla would have done.

So maybe Kira and Marla weren't as much alike as Cutty had thought.

And maybe given the fact that Kira had that softer side, that Kira *could* be persuaded to temporarily ignore a little debris in favor of the people in her life, made it easier to overlook those times when she was in a frenzy over a minor detail.

Cutty unwrapped his cast and limped to the sink to shave, thinking as he did about the way he'd felt when he first woke up this morning. The way he'd felt more and more the longer Kira was around.

Genuine, deep-rooted happiness.

Was that feeling worth the times when Kira was a little nuts?

It must have been, because there he was, lathering his face with shaving foam and grinning as that feeling washed through him again.

As that feeling washed through him again at the thought of having Kira around *all* the time to make him continue to feel that way.

Did he want her to be around all the time? he asked himself.

But that was a no-brainer. He sure as hell didn't want her to leave. He sure as hell didn't want to lose her or this feeling.

"So you take the good with the bad," he told his reflection.

But that wasn't really fair, either. Because the *bad* wasn't really bad, now that he thought about it. Sure, Kira had come across the yard at the crack of dawn in the mornings to try to get a head start on keeping an impeccable house. But she hadn't roused him out of bed to do it, too. The way Marla would have.

Sure, Kira had strived for perfection, but she hadn't been so obsessed with it that she'd made things around there miserable by demanding that he meet her unreasonable standards, too. The way Marla had.

Sure, Kira had *wanted* things to be tidier and more orderly, but if they weren't she had still been capable of separating herself from it long enough to have a good time—to sit and talk with him at the end of the day, to go to his birthday party, to go to the awards ceremony and the softball game, to play with the babies. And to let him do all those things, too. Without guilt. Without berating him and making him feel guilty for it. And that wasn't at all like Marla, either.

In fact, Cutty thought sadly, he didn't think Marla had ever really found much joy in anything.

And the truth was, she'd ridden him so hard she'd taken all the joy out of him, too.

Joy that Kira had put back.

So, no, the *bad* part that went with the good of Kira wasn't really all that bad. It was really just a matter of her being harder on herself than on anyone else.

And the good part? That wasn't just good, either. It was great. It made him happy. *Genuinely* happy.

Happy enough to want to hang on to her.

Even if she did periodically freak out over how much dust there was on the coffee table and who might see it.

Kira was what he wanted.

Kira and that joy and genuine, deep-rooted happiness that only she brought him.

And suddenly, as he took his cane and went back into his bedroom to put on a pair of jeans and a T-shirt, he decided he was going to do something about it.

Kira had just gotten the twins into their high chairs for lunch when Betty arrived.

"My aunt got here early, so I thought I'd come right away," the older woman announced.

For once Kira was glad for the distraction of the housekeeper and nanny. Cutty had only joined Kira and the girls about an hour earlier, but for Kira it had been an awkward hour.

Making love the night before had changed things, and she wasn't exactly sure how to behave. There they were, just like every other day since she'd come to Northbridge except that now she didn't know what to expect. She didn't know if they should talk about what had happened or pretend it *hadn't* happened, or what.

And Cutty was no help. He was being particularly quiet, and she kept catching him watching her all the while she was straightening up the living room and trying to entertain the girls.

Betty hadn't been in the house ten minutes when she started her usual commentary on the wonders of Marla and where Marla liked this and that, and how Marla would have done what Kira was apparently doing wrong when she gave Mel and Mandy slices of bologna to munch on rather than cutting the lunch meat into pieces for them.

But the older woman was barely getting warmed up when Cutty came into the kitchen and said, "Think you can handle this on your own for a while, Betty?"

"That's what I'm here for," Betty answered, seeming thrilled to take over for Kira, who was surprised by the request. And confused and curious about it, too.

Cutty took her hand then—shocking her even more by the display of familiarity—and led her out the back door.

In the direction of the garage apartment.

But surely he couldn't be going there, she thought. He couldn't be thinking of repeating the lovemaking of the night before. Not in the middle of the day, with Betty only a backyard away.

The garage apartment was just where Cutty was headed, though, and within moments Kira found herself behind closed doors.

Where the bed hadn't yet been made.

Just the sight of it did two things to Kira—it gave her an instant flash of vivid memory of what they'd done there and also inspired a sharp desire to do it again.

But if that really was what Cutty had in mind, she just couldn't do it, so she turned her back to the bed and faced him with a questioning glance.

Cutty was perceptive enough to catch it and even to know what was on her mind.

He smiled a one-sided smile and said, ''Do you honestly think I brought you out here to ravage you in broad daylight while Betty baby-sits?''

''I hope not,'' Kira admitted.

''You can relax, that's not what I have up my sleeve. Much as I wish it was.''

Kira refrained from saying *me, too.* ''What *do* you have up your sleeve?''

''I wanted to talk to you. Without anyone overhearing. In all the birthday commotion yesterday and last night we never got into what's going to happen now that Betty is coming back to work.''

''No, we didn't,'' Kira agreed, although the subject had been weighing on her.

''Well, we need to talk about it.''

''Okay,'' Kira said, waiting to hear what he had to say.

He came to stand close in front of her, reaching a hand to her arm. A hand that sent ripples of wonderful sense memory all through her and made it difficult to concentrate on what he was saying.

But she put some effort into it in time to hear, ''I woke up this morning feeling incredible. And I realized that you're the reason.''

Kira couldn't help smiling. "I'm glad."

"I also realized that with Betty coming back it could mean that you might not stick around much longer and the thought of you leaving was…" Cutty chuckled wryly and shook his head. "Well, I didn't like it."

The man knew how to make her feel pretty darn good, too. In more ways than one.

But she didn't say that. Instead she made a joke. "So what do you want to do? Hire me on as your own private microbiologist?"

"I want you here, that's for sure," Cutty said in answer to her jest. But he wasn't kidding. He was serious.

"I thought a lot about it this morning," he went on. "I know you came to find the twins, that you only stayed to help out and to get to know them, to start to build a relationship with them. But in the meantime you've also built a relationship with me. A pretty terrific one, I think. And I don't want this to be all there is to it."

Kira didn't know what *this* entailed. But she was beginning to have nervous butterflies in her stomach and she tried to calm them as he continued.

"You know, when you first showed up here I expected you to be just like Marla. I figured the house—and the girls and I for that matter—would be whipped into the kind of shape Tom Wentworth would have been proud of. I definitely didn't think I'd have someone sitting with me at the end of the day, or going to the softball game, or my birthday party, or someone who would be playing with the girls.''

Those good feelings began to fade in Kira because to her that seemed on the brink of criticism. The kind of criticism her father would have dished out—although more harshly—for slacking off when there was work to be done.

''But I finally came to realize,'' Cutty was saying, ''that you're different from Marla. That in some ways you really aren't Tom Wentworth's daughter. That only Marla was. And I guess it finally sank into my head that that part of my life is over. That it's time to move on, to start fresh—all those platitudes that are making a lot of sense to me today. So I just want to know if we can work this out.''

Kira wasn't sure what he meant by *work this out,* either. But her confusion wasn't what was uppermost in her mind. What *was* uppermost in her mind was what he'd said about her being different than Marla. To her, being different than Marla meant not as good as Marla....

And suddenly it seemed very important that it had been Ad who had said Cutty and Marla's marriage had been troubled, that it hadn't been Cutty himself who had told her. And that maybe, looking in from the sidelines, Ad had been wrong. That the way Marla had done things was the way Cutty had liked it. Or at least what he expected.

What had he said? she wondered suddenly when it occurred to her that her own thoughts had interrupted the course of this conversation. He wanted to know if they could work this out.

"I'm sure we can work out when I come to Northbridge to see the girls and other times when they can come to Denver to be with me, so you can have some freedom to get on with your life," she said, interpreting what he meant while her mind was still really on the idea that Cutty, of all people, had compared her unfavorably with her sister.

He frowned at her, his expression confused now. "I wasn't talking about visitation with the twins," he said as if he'd thought that was perfectly clear. "I was talking about you and me. About you staying."

"Staying? I don't know how I could stay," she said, trying to ward off the hurt that was beginning inside her and wondering if there would ever be a time when she wouldn't be in her sister's shadow. "I have my apartment and my job teaching at the university—"

"So give up your apartment and get a teaching job at Northbridge College. I know it wouldn't be as prestigious as working at a university and it probably wouldn't pay quite as well, but I have some influence with the powers that be and I'm sure I could get you onto the staff."

And not because of her own merits. Because of who he was and probably because the dean and the board of directors had all thought so highly of Marla that they would hire her sister...

"I don't want to get a job that way. I got the one

I have because I'm known for my work, for my accomplishments.''

"Then your credentials will get you on here, too," Cutty countered as if it were inconsequential. "I'm just saying—"

Kira cut him off with a resounding no. "I can't stay in Northbridge."

"I don't know why not," Cutty protested, taking his hand away from her arm.

"I just can't, that's all. I won't," Kira said firmly as she endured the regret that washed through her at losing his touch.

Cutty frowned a confused frown. "What did I miss here? I thought...especially after last night—"

"Last night was...nice." And that was a vast understatement. "But it can't change the whole course of my future. I can't give up everything I've worked for and accomplished just because of it."

"I'm only asking you to consider making a few adjustments to have what you said you came here to find in the first place—family."

"The twins will still be my family." The twins who never knew Marla, who would never compare her to Marla, who would always take her only for who she was on her own.

"The twins," Cutty parroted as if that clarified something for him. Something that struck a blow.

But Kira forced herself to stand her ground by reminding herself of all the times she'd thought *Marla's house, Marla's things*. By the idea of living with so many people like Betty and Carol the saleswoman and so many others she'd met while she'd been in North-bridge who couldn't see her for anything but Marla's sister. By remembering that Cutty thought she paled in comparison, too...

Despite the ache that was rapidly wrapping around her heart, she said, "I guess really, since Betty is back and you don't need me anymore I should probably just go ahead and pack my things to go home."

Cutty's deep green eyes were piercing as he stared at her. "I can't believe this."

"There's nothing to not believe. I worked hard to get my degree, to get my teaching job. I had some free time to come here and now I'll go back."

"As if your degrees and job are more important?"

"They might not be important to you, but they are to me."

"More important than anything—or anyone—else? Like a true daughter of Tom Wentworth?" Cutty shook his head again. "You've either fooled the hell out of me since you got here or you're fooling your-self right now."

Kira didn't understand that, either. But he'd struck a blow of his own with that *daughter of Tom Went-worth* remark and so she merely raised her chin de-fiantly, leaving him to think whatever it was he was thinking while she fought to keep from breaking down and letting him know how difficult this was, how much she wished it could all be different, how much it was hurting her.

Then she said, "I'll pack and say goodbye to the girls and be out by the end of the day."

"No!" Cutty nearly shouted. "How did we go from everything being okay when I brought you in here, to you being gone by the end of the day?"

Kira couldn't go on looking at that handsome face, at that body she'd been so intimate with such a short time before, and stick to her guns. So she turned her back to him and said, "It's for the best. Betty is back and can handle everything. The girls love her. I might as well get home."

"This doesn't even make sense. What did I do? What didn't I do? Or say? Or... One minute we're going along great—better than great—and the next minute not only aren't you staying, you're leaving right away?"

"I just think it's for the best," she said quietly, around a throat full of tears.

"And you're just going to let me hang, wondering what the hell went wrong in the last ten minutes?"

"Nothing went wrong," she said because she couldn't tell him the truth about what she felt, about how much of a mistake it had been for her to put herself in a position where she was being compared with her sister once again. About how much of a mistake she knew it would be to put herself into that position forever. "We just see things differently."

"Apparently," Cutty said sarcastically.

For a long moment neither of them said anything at all, and in the silence Kira fought not to cry.

Then Cutty said, "So that's it? You're really going?"

Kira could only nod confirmation.

A few more minutes of that tense silence passed and then Cutty said, "I'll never understand this."

But he must have given up trying to because then Kira heard the apartment door open and he was gone.

Chapter Nine

It was two o'clock the next morning when a weary Kira unlocked the door to her Denver apartment. She turned on the table lamp just to the right of the threshold and carried her overfilled suitcase in before she noticed her best friend Kit on her couch.

Kit had obviously been asleep, but with Kira's entrance she sat up and squinted against the sudden light. "Hi," she said simply enough, as if her being there like that wasn't an unusual occurrence.

"Hi," Kira answered with a question in her tone as she closed the door behind her. "How come you're sleeping on my couch?"

"You sounded so bad when you called that I wanted to be here when you got home," Kit explained.

Kira had called from the Billings Airport early in the evening and although she hadn't given Kit any of the details, she had told her things had taken a turn for the worse with Cutty. She also hadn't been able to conceal how upset she was.

"You didn't have to do that," she said. But she was glad Kit had. Despite the hour, Kira knew she wouldn't be able to sleep and she really didn't want to be alone.

"I brought cake," her friend said. "Chocolate fudge. Guaranteed to lift the deepest doldrums."

Kira made an attempt to smile. "Thanks but I don't think I can even eat that right now."

Under Kit's scrutiny, Kira turned on another lamp, kicked off her shoes and dropped into the matching plaid armchair that was positioned at a forty-five degree angle to the sofa.

"You look awful," Kit observed. "You cried all the way home, didn't you?"

"I tried not to but I couldn't seem to help it. It was embarrassing. The woman next to me on the plane thought I must be going to a funeral."

"Tell me what happened."

First Kira told Kit how good things had gotten between herself and Cutty since she'd talked to Kit on the phone on Sunday. She told her about everything Ad had said about Marla, and about Cutty and Marla's marriage. She told her about sleeping with Cutty after his birthday party. And then she told her about what had happened the morning after the party.

Kit listened without saying much, letting Kira pour

it all out. At one point, she did get up and go into the bathroom to bring back a box of tissues so Kira could blow her nose and mop at the tears that just kept coming, though.

"So here I am," Kira concluded when she'd finished. "I just left. I packed up and went back into the house to say goodbye to the twins—"

"That couldn't have been easy," Kit interjected.

Proving her friend's point, the tears Kira had gotten under control began to run down her cheeks again. "It was horrible. I just wanted to pick them up and run with them. But at least Cutty was upstairs so I didn't have to see him again. I don't think I could have survived it."

"How about a cup of tea?" Kit offered.

Kira nodded her agreement as she blew her nose yet again.

Kit went around the island counter that separated the tiny studio apartment into living-sleeping space and kitchen, and made the tea. By the time she returned, Kira had managed to stop crying again.

Kit handed her a mug and then took her own with her to sit on the couch again.

After a few sips, Kit said, "Tell me again *exactly* what Cutty said about Marla."

"He said that he expected me to be like her," Kira complied with a hint of anger in her voice. "He thought I'd whip everything into the kind of shape my father would have been proud of, and that he hadn't thought I would end up sitting around or going to a softball game or a birthday party or that I'd play with the twins instead of doing the work that needed to be done.''

Kit frowned at that. ''But when we talked on Sunday didn't you say that he kept encouraging you to leave things until the next day and not to worry about what didn't get done?''

''Yes. But maybe it was some kind of test or maybe he didn't really mean it or something.''

''You think it was a trap?'' Kit asked.

''I guess not. But I don't know why he said that kind of thing all along and then held it against me when that's what I did.''

''Are you sure he *was* holding it against you?'' Kit asked kindly.

''What do you mean? What else could he have meant?''

''I'm on your side, Kira. I really am. I'm behind you a hundred percent. It's just that I'm also wondering if you took some of what he said at the end differently than he might have intended it.''

But rather than pursuing what Kit was suggesting, Kira seized the one word that spurred her memory. ''*Different*—that's the other thing he said—he said he finally realized I was different than Marla. That I wasn't really Tom Wentworth's daughter the way Marla was.''

''But, Kira, isn't that a *good* thing?'' Kit asked somewhat cautiously. ''That's what I was getting at— what I hear in that isn't bad. You know he didn't care for your father. That he thought he was a tyrant— which, by the way, from what you said Cutty's friend told you, sounds like what Marla was, too. It seems to me that it's a compliment that Cutty thought Marla was like your father and you aren't.''

That was definitely a different point of view. One Kira hadn't considered.

But Kit continued before she had a chance to confirm or deny it.

''And as for you thinking Cutty was criticizing you for sitting around or going out or playing with the babies rather than doing housework—maybe he was saying that was better than the way it had been with your sister who wouldn't have even gone to a birthday party for him.''

''Don't forget, though, it wasn't Cutty who said Marla had done anything wrong. It was his friend,'' Kira said, defending her interpretation even as a spark of hope sprang to life that Kit might be right.

Kit had an answer for that, too. ''His friend also told you that Cutty *wouldn't* say anything against her—especially to you. And unless I'm missing something, Cutty never said anything particularly positive about Marla. He also wasn't the one who threw it up to you that she'd done things better than you were doing. That all came from that Betty person. The same as all Marla's accolades came from people on the outside. It was also that Betty who acted the way your father did with your mother about making sure everything of Marla's was kept just the way she left it.''

That was actually true, Kira realized when she thought about it. It *had* always been Betty and outside people who had touted the glories of Marla. It hadn't been Cutty.

Still, she didn't think she could have been so wrong and she tried hard to remember a time when Cutty had insisted that things be kept the way Marla had kept them, or that Kira had to do anything the way Marla had.

The problem was, no matter how hard she tried, she couldn't come up with a single instance.

In fact, it suddenly occurred to her that after her first disastrous day of trying to take care of the house and the twins he'd actually told her she needed to have *less* concern for doing things the way Marla had. And even when she'd broken Marla's favorite vase, Cutty had taken it in stride. It had been Betty who had made Kira feel bad about it.

And when it came to keeping Marla's memory alive the way Kira's father had kept his first wife's memory alive? Cutty couldn't be accused of that when he hadn't even wanted to talk about Marla.

Which could also have been some of the reason Cutty hadn't been the one to tell her about the way things had been in his marriage…

Kira closed her eyes as everything Kit had brought to her attention began to sink in. "Do you think I just jumped the gun because of my own warped competition with Marla?" she asked her friend.

"I think you heard what Cutty said and saw things with competition coloring it, yes," Kit admitted tactfully. "I just think you've spent so much of your life being compared to Marla and feeling like she was the standard you had to live up to that it's hard for you to see it any other way. I also think that this time around you might have won the competition—in Cutty's view at least—but that you're so used to believing you're not as good as Marla that you didn't recognize it.''

Kira had opened her eyes again to look at her friend. ''But that's another thing, Kit—even if I won the competition in Cutty's view, and even if Ad had reservations about Marla, there's still Betty and a whole town full of people who adored Marla and never saw me for myself. Do I really want to even consider being in a place where the general consensus will be that I'm not as good?''

''I'm not thrilled about even the possibility of you moving,'' Kit qualified, ''but who cares what anybody thinks? There's a great guy who you're crazy about and who seems crazy about you, and two babies you adore who adore you back—why would it matter what anyone else thinks? Maybe in that you are being too much like Marla and your father.''

Kira laughed a small, humorless laugh. ''So what it all boils down to is that you just think I've been an idiot and that I've completely blown something that could have been the best thing that ever happened to me?''

''You know I don't think you're an idiot. I think that you just saw this from a perspective based on your own experiences. We all do that. But I also think that you should get some sleep and then call this guy and talk to him, find out if I'm right or if you are. What harm is there in that?''

After only about two hours of sleep Kira did more than merely call Cutty the way Kit had advised. She caught a plane to Montana, rented another car and was within a few miles of Northbridge again by three o'clock the following afternoon.

She was also wondering if she'd just gone off the deep end to be doing this.

But she pushed that thought out of her mind and forced herself to focus only on the reason she'd done this in the first place—to see if she honestly had a chance with Cutty.

Because once Kit had left her alone, Kira had still had trouble falling asleep and in that time before she had, she'd thought a lot about all her friend had said. She'd also thought a lot about what Ad had told her. And she'd thought a *whole* lot about Cutty.

What she'd realized was that Kit really might be right and that she might have been wrong in just about everything that had caused her to make her decision to leave Northbridge and Cutty and the twins behind.

Because despite going over and over almost every moment she'd had with Cutty she still couldn't think of even one time when he'd criticized her. She couldn't think of even one time when he'd compared her to Marla. One time when he'd told her she had to do anything the way Marla had done it.

And as for the feelings the other people in North-bridge had for Marla? Sometime around four that morning Kira had decided that was something belonging to Marla. That love, that respect, that admiration her sister had worked hard to achieve *shouldn't* be challenged. It should be left to Marla and Marla's memory. Especially when it had come at what might have been a very high cost.

And more important, for the first time in Kira's life, she'd come to realize that she really could be free of the shadow cast by Marla if she stopped comparing herself to her sister. If she stopped expecting herself to live up to her. She'd realized that Kit was right when she'd said that what a whole lot of other people thought wasn't the issue if *she* didn't think she was somehow less than Marla. Certainly what other people thought shouldn't have the power to influence her or her decisions when it came to Cutty or the twins.

Because as long as it wasn't Cutty who was determined to keep Marla alive—the way Tom Wentworth had tried to keep his first wife alive—as long as it wasn't Cutty who was comparing Kira to Marla, then nothing else mattered.

Except maybe if Kira's response the day before had closed whatever door Cutty had been opening for her. *That* was definitely something that would matter…

The gas station Kira had stopped at for directions the first time she'd arrived in Northbridge came into view just then and knowing how close she was to Cutty's house set off butterflies in her stomach.

What if Kit was wrong and I was right, though…

That thought had flashed through her mind a dozen

times on the return trip, and she'd dismissed it. Only suddenly it wasn't as easy to shake.

What *if* Cutty had been saying he accepted the fact that she wasn't as good as Marla but he wanted to work things out with her anyway? And what exactly did *working things out* entail? Had he wanted her to just stay in Northbridge in general? Or in the garage apartment? Or had he been talking about more than that?

"You're here to clear everything up," she reminded herself. "*Then* you'll make a decision. If he isn't offering what you want, you can just say no and go back to Denver."

That was how she'd gotten up the courage to do this at all—she'd decided she was just going to go back to Northbridge, find out exactly what Cutty had meant the previous morning, and then—and only then—would she make up her mind what she wanted to do.

Kira pulled up to the curb in front of Cutty's house.

She couldn't take her eyes off it as she fumbled to turn off the engine in the unfamiliar car.

Betty would probably be there, she knew, and she didn't relish facing the woman after the quick, tearful goodbye to the twins that the other woman had witnessed the day before.

But she hadn't come all this way to chicken out just because Betty made her nervous and so she took the key out of the ignition, slipped from behind the wheel and headed for the house with her heart beating a mile a minute.

The front door was open, just as it had been the first time she'd climbed those porch steps. But now Cutty wasn't at the hall table, talking on the phone. She spotted him through the picture window, sitting on the sofa with his leg propped on a pillow on the coffee table.

She didn't hear the sound of the television or even the radio or stereo and he seemed to be just staring into space. With a very dour expression on his handsome, clean-shaven face.

He spied her then and the dour expression transformed instantly into one of surprise. Surprise that got him off the couch in a hurry so that he reached the front screen when she did.

For a brief, fleeting moment Kira wondered if he was going to slam the door in her face and lock it to keep her out.

But that wasn't what he did.

He pushed the screen open wide and said a tentative, questioning, "Hi."

"Hi," Kira responded the same way.

"You're about the last person I expected to see," Cutty informed her. "Come in."

Kira did, thinking that no man should be allowed to look that good in a plain pair of jeans and a white T-shirt, and that if she ended up having to turn around and leave him again it was going to be even harder than it had been the day before.

From the entryway inside, Kira glanced around in search of the twins and Betty, but she didn't see or hear anything that gave her a clue as to where they were.

"Betty took the girls to the park. You just missed them," Cutty said, guessing what she was looking for.

"Good," Kira said. "Then we can talk."

Cutty motioned with his cane toward the living room and Kira went ahead of him, keeping her fingers crossed that she hadn't made a mistake by coming here and thinking that maybe Kit had been as right about doing this over the phone as Kira hoped her friend had been about everything else.

But it was too late now and so all she could do was go through with what she'd come for.

Nervous, though, she began to pick up the few toys that were on the floor.

"I thought you came to talk?" Cutty said from behind her.

Kira dropped the toys into the toy box and turned back to find him still standing, his weight braced on the cane, watching her.

Now or never...

"I did."

"What do you want to talk about?"

Kira screwed up her courage and said, "I need to know if I misunderstood what you said to me yesterday morning."

Cutty's frown was dark and intense. "I thought I made myself pretty clear. I asked you to stay. You said no."

And obviously he wasn't only confused the way he had been at the time. He was angry now, as well.

"What you said about my staying wasn't altogether clear, either. But maybe we can get into that after you explain the rest of what you said."

"The rest?"

Kira took a deep, fortifying breath. "This is what I thought you were saying to me—" She went on to tell him the way she'd taken what he'd said. Honestly. Openly. Sparing nothing, including the depth of her own insecurities when it came to being compared to her sister and the need that had been ingrained in her to do everything she could to be as good, to excel.

The longer she talked the more Cutty's expression and stance relaxed until, by the time she was finished, his eyebrows were arched in disbelief.

"You are so far off the mark," he said then in regards to what she believed he'd been telling her the previous day. "I know Ad told you how things were between Marla and me—he confessed that last night. He said he did it because he knew I'd never tell you myself and he was right. I wouldn't have. But not because it isn't all true. I won't say anything against Marla because she's gone and everything that happened, everything she was and did, is over. Nothing can be served by rehashing it. Plus she needed so badly for people to think of her the way they did— the way they do—I couldn't ruin that for her when she was alive and I can't do it to her memory, either."

Kira had to admire his loyalty even if it had tweaked those insecurities of hers. But she still needed to know just how true what Ad had said was.

"So the marriage wasn't all Betty and everyone else around here believes it was?"

"Had Marla not turned up pregnant we probably wouldn't have even *dated* another month, Kira. We were just teenagers. No, the marriage that came out of that wasn't what people think it was. When you first showed up here and offered to help out, all I could think was that you were bound to be like Marla and I couldn't get into that again. So your friend was right—I was thrilled to figure out that the biggest part of you *is* different from Marla. I was *glad* that you were willing to overlook a few things to go to the game and the party and the awards ceremony with me. And the fact that you were playing with the twins when I expected you to be working like mad to make everything perfect before Betty came back? That's what made me realize I wanted you to stay."

Relief washed through Kira so thoroughly she almost felt weak. But at the same time there was that *stay* part again and she still didn't know what, exactly, he had in mind.

"Now explain what you mean when you say that you want me to stay," she said more bravely.

A slow, sexy smile brightened his features and he used the head of his cane to hook her upper arm and pull her to stand close in front of him.

"I really didn't make myself clear yesterday, did I?" he said. "*Stay* means I want you to move to Northbridge and marry me. It means I want you to be Mel and Mandy's mom, and I want to have a couple more kids with you. It means I want to spend every day for the rest of my life with you. It means—'' he was suddenly giving special enunciation to each word ''—that I'm so in love with you that I'm damn near giddy.''

It was Kira's turn to smile. ''And you can live with your whole town probably thinking you've traded down?''

''They're all going to love you as much as I do,'' Cutty assured. ''And one way or another, the only thing I care about is you saying a big fat yes to being my wife.''

There was one more thing Kira had thought about when she'd considered the possibility of a future with Cutty and she thought she had to say it now. But she was reluctant to and it must have shown on her face because he said, ''What? You're going to say no?''

''I have just one condition,'' she ventured. ''But it's a huge one.''

''Let's hear it?''

''The whole time I was here I just kept thinking that this is Marla's house, that everything in it is Marla's.''

''And you don't want to live in Marla's house with Marla's things,'' Cutty guessed.

Kira grimaced. ''I'm sorry. I know this is your home, too, and they're your things, too. But—''

Cutty chuckled slightly. ''Gone!''

''Me? Or the house and the things?''

''Not you. The house and the things. You're more important to me than all of it. I think we *should* start fresh. Although I will have to keep Mel and Mandy,'' he joked.

Kira laughed as even more relief flooded her. ''I wouldn't give them up for anything.''

''So where's the big fat yes to marrying me?''

''Big fat yes!'' she repeated with enthusiasm.

Cutty pulled her the rest of the way into his arms then and kissed her a kiss that initially just seemed to put a stamp on the deal.

But it took only a few moments for the kiss to become more than that. To rekindle what they'd shared after Cutty's birthday party and ignite a desire hotter than the sun.

Cutty stopped then and glanced at the clock on the fireplace mantel. ''Hmm. You know, we might have half an hour yet to ourselves.''

Kira knew what was going through his mind and she merely smiled.

But apparently it was enough consent for Cutty because without another word he took her hand and led her through the kitchen and out the back door, all the way to the garage apartment where Kira had stripped and remade the bed before she'd left for Denver.

With time limited, they didn't waste any of it.

Clothes were shed as mouths clung and then Cutty laid Kira back on the mattress where a passion even greater than what they'd shared before erupted.

There were no inhibitions. There was no timidity. Hands explored and aroused. Lips parted and tongues teased and tormented and claimed each other. Bodies came together in one graceful motion and moved like the rhythm of ship and sea to reach an all-new height, to find a glorious, unguarded ecstasy that left them breathlessly holding each other as Cutty rolled them to their sides and pressed tender lips to the top of her head.

"It's a good thing you said yes or I think I'd just keep you prisoner out here for the rest of your life," he said after a moment, his voice raspy with the remnants of lovemaking so divine Kira felt as if she were floating on air.

"What would I be? Your love-slave?" she asked.

He grinned a satiated grin. "Love-slave," he repeated as if trying out the sound of it. "I like that."

"But think of the scandal when, one day, Betty happened upon me handcuffed to the bed. Small Town Cop Keeps Microbiologist For His Own Personal Pleasure," Kira said as if reciting a headline.

"You'd have sympathy in your favor, though, and the whole town would make you its new idol."

Kira laughed, realizing just how unimportant that seemed now, in Cutty's arms, knowing he was hers. "That's okay. I think being your wife will be enough for me."

He reared back to look into her eyes and his expression surprised her because it seemed that her simple comment had genuinely moved him.

"I hope so," he said softly.

Kira pressed one palm to the side of that face she knew she'd never tire of and kissed him. "I love you, Cutty," she said then, her own full heart echoing in her voice.

"I love you, too. More than I even knew until you walked out of here yesterday. Don't ever do that again."

"You're going to have to get a court order if you want to get rid of me," she told him.

Commotion from inside the house then let them know Betty was back with the twins.

"We should get up and get dressed before she catches us," Kira said.

Cutty grinned. "Yeah, I suppose we should," he agreed as he kissed her one more time.

Then they both made quick work of dressing and finger-combing hair and making sure all evidence of how they'd spent that half hour was concealed.

But regardless of how concealed it was, Kira carried with her the warm glow left by that and by the knowledge that she'd finally found her own heart's true desire. Her own heart's true love. That she'd found it in Cutty.

And that along with him came two beautiful babies she couldn't have loved more if she'd given birth to them herself.

Two beautiful babies who were just a wonderful bonus to make her life complete.

* * * * *

Look for Victoria Pade's next
NORTHBRIDGE NUPTIALS *book,*
WEDDING WILLIES,
in August 2004, only from
Silhouette Special Edition.

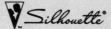

SPECIAL EDITION™

From bestselling author

Victoria Pade

Northbridge Nuptials

Where a walk down the aisle is never far behind.

BABIES IN THE BARGAIN

(Silhouette Special Edition #1623,
on-sale July 2004)

WEDDING WILLIES

(Silhouette Special Edition #1628,
on-sale August 2004)

And later this year...

HAVING THE
BACHELOR'S BABY

Available at your favorite retail outlet.

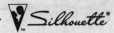

SPECIAL EDITION™

From bestselling author

VICTORIA PADE

Northbridge Nuptials

Where a walk down the aisle is never far behind.

Wedding Willies

(Silhouette Special Edition #1628)

Although she's famous for bailing on two of her own trips to the altar, Kit McIntyre has no problem being part of her best friend's happy day. But when she's forced to spend lots of one-on-one time with the sexy best man, Ad Walker, Kit's eyes are finally opened to the very real possibility of happily-ever-after.

*Available August 2004
at your favorite retail outlet.*

And coming in January 2005,
don't miss Book Three, ***Having the Bachelor's Baby.***

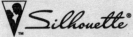
COMING NEXT MONTH

SPECIAL EDITION